A BOO-TIFUL TRICK!

On the wall was a hooded ghost about ten feet tall with sunken eyes and long, knobby hands. I wanted to run away, but I was afraid the ghost would catch me.

"Who is it?" I whispered desperately.

Then came a groan that sounded like a roar.

"Hello?" I yelled.

There was a clank of chains. Next the clanking was replaced by a voice. A loud, frightening voice . . .

"Scooooottttttiiieeee. . . ."

My mouth fell open.

"Sco . . . Sco . . . Sco . . ." It suddenly sounded scratchy. Like a record player that was stuck in one spot.

Then I knew. There was no tall ghost on the wall. I got up and looked at my record player. There was a record on it called "Sound Effects for Ghosts." No one had really been yelling Scottie.

I had been tricked. By a ghost.

"Malcolm?" I asked softly.

"None other," came a voice. "Long time no see, my boy!"

Bantam Skylark Books of related interest
Ask your bookseller for the books you have missed

Ghost A La Mode

Judi Miller

A BANTAM SKYLARK BOOK®

NEW YORK · TORONTO · LONDON · SYDNEY · AUCKLAND

RL 3, 008–012

GHOST A LA MODE

A Bantam Skylark Book / October 1989

Skylark Books is a registered trademark of Bantam Books, a division of Bantam Doubleday Dell Publishing Group, Inc. Registered in U.S. Patent and Trademark Office and elsewhere.

ISBN 0-553-15755-8

Published simultaneously in the United States and Canada

Bantam Books are published by Bantam Books, a division of Bantam Doubleday Dell Publishing Group, Inc. Its trademark, consisting of the words "Bantam Books" and the portrayal of a rooster, is Registered in U.S. Patent and Trademark Office and in other countries. Marca Registrada. Bantam Books, 666 Fifth Avenue, New York, New York 10103.

PRINTED IN THE UNITED STATES OF AMERICA

O   0 9 8 7 6 5 4 3 2 1

To my cousin Bobbie who taught me
all about ghosts

1

Initiation Rites

There was a full moon that night. I was lucky because I had forgotten to steal a flashlight before sneaking out of the house. I would have been very scared walking all alone in the dark. But I was scared anyway for another reason. I was about to be initiated into the Panthers!

I began to follow the instructions the leader of the Panthers, Big Mikey, had given me over the phone during the most important call of my life.

I still couldn't believe they'd voted me in. It wasn't as if I was friends with any of those guys or anything. Me, Scott Sheldon! I was about to go from the invisible kid from the fifth grade to one of eight boys in one of the coolest, most popular clubs at Jefferson Grammar School.

That is, if I made it through initiation.

I studied the directions, walked two blocks, and turned left at the big oak tree where people carved their initials. Next, I was to hang a left and take the gravel path behind Mr. Neubert's old wreck of a barn.

1

There were a lot of barns in Chagrin Falls, Ohio, where I had been living since the middle of the summer. We moved here from Mayfield Heights, Ohio, where I had lived from the time I was born. Some of the barns were decorated and were just for show. Except the only show Mr. Neubert's barn could have been decorated for was a spook show.

I took a deep breath and bolted down that gravel path. When I reached the abandoned gas station, it took me about five minutes to stop panting and shaking. Boy, was I lucky none of the guys were there yet. I walked over to the dismantled soda pop machine. My instructions said I was supposed to stand by the machine and bark like a dog.

Did I write that down right? Bark like a dog? I wouldn't have made that up. Mikey must have told me to do that. Then he'd said after the ritual barking I'd be picked up by a soon-to-be fellow Panther.

I couldn't believe my luck. Two days ago Big Mikey, the most popular boy in school, called me and asked me to play football with the guys. Today he called me and invited me into the club. He said this way I'd be officially one of the guys. In one bark I would soon be one of the coolest guys in the school.

I barked.

Someone appeared.

I barked again. Actually, I was pretty good at imitations.

A hand clasped over my eyes from the back.

"Scottie Feldon?"

I shook my head. The hand came away.

"Close," I said. "Scottie Sheldon."

"Follow me," he said. Now that was kind of hard, because the boy, Richie Silver, who sat behind me in music, had put a blindfold over my eyes. I crashed right into a tree. And then he guided me up a rope ladder. A tree house? My knees were shaking, but I made it.

When the blindfold was taken off I saw it was a really nice, really large tree-clubhouse. The six boys Mikey and I played football with were all there. They were all Panthers. Three were in my class. There was one other boy I'd never seen before. All seven were glaring angrily at me.

I broke out into a cold sweat. What had I done to get them so mad?

Big Mikey said, "Scottie Sheldon's the new Panther."

There was no answer.

"Hi, everyone," I said. But my voice was high and squeaky. Except for Big Mikey no one gave me what you would call a big welcome. Though I was sure glad to be there. I decided it was because they were cool that they acted like that.

Then Richie said, "He'll have to have a name."

All the boys nodded.

"We have special club names," said Big Mikey. "Mine's Big Buster."

They went through their club names one at a time. I listened carefully because I knew I'd better remember them. Patch, Skip, Tiger, Rags, Duke, Brutus, and Sharkey.

I almost shouted with relief. I thought the names were going to be really weird. But they sounded like dog names. Weren't they supposed to be Panthers?

"I guess you can call me Rover," I said.

"Good name," Kevin, one of the boys in my class, commented.

"So that's it," Big Mikey said.

"That's it?" I asked. "I was told over the phone there would be an initiation."

"Oh, right," Joey said. "Usually we make a kid drink four pints of fresh pigeon blood and then we send him door-to-door to ask people if they know there are vampires in the neighborhood. And we follow to make sure the kid's really doing it." He snickered.

They couldn't really make you drink that, I thought. Could they?

Big Mikey said, "Aw, right. We'll just have Scottie swear in because it's getting real late."

I took the Panthers oath by repeating after Big Mikey mostly stuff about being able to keep a secret. Then he handed me a gray sweatshirt with my name embroidered on it in red and black. I looked up at Big Mikey. And then I put it on. I didn't care that it was a little big.

Petey said, "It used to belong to Freddie, but he moved to Chicago."

"Gee, well, it's great to be a Panther. I'm really

glad I was asked in." I hoped I didn't sound as happy as I really felt. That wouldn't be cool.

"Hey it's getting late," Jeff said. Jeff was tall. He was a great basketball player.

"Yeah, I gotta get home before they miss me. It's my grandmother's birthday," Tiger said. No, it was Patch. But it was really Blake.

"Okay, Scott," Big Mikey said. Everyone scrambled down the ladder. I went down shakily, but just as fast as the guys, my fellow Panthers.

I was feeling great. For the longest time they hadn't included me in their football games. But now I'd never be left out again, I thought happily.

One of the guys stopped to talk. Tiger. Also known in the fifth grade as Todd. "Listen, you're automatically popular when you're a Panther, Scott. It opens doors. It gets you on all the good teams in gym. Most of the time they elect you captain. Especially if you have your sweatshirt on. Well, I gotta run and catch up with the other guys."

I nodded and watched him run. I had never been so far from home alone this late at night. I wondered if my parents had figured out I wasn't in my room.

When I'd left the house, my mom was settling in for one of her two-hour telephone calls. My dad was almost asleep in front of the TV. I was sure they didn't miss me yet, but I started to run anyway. The moonlight cast eerie shadows, especially around Mr.

Neubert's barn. I was too happy to be scared, though.

Goodbye, invisible kid. I was in a club and I was in the best one! Then I thought about Howard Fierman, the only boy who'd been willing to be my friend. Until now, that is. Could I be cool and still be friendly with Howard?

See, Howard has this really disgusting habit. He picks his nose and eats it. Yucch!

I looked down and pinched my sweatshirt. Yeah, it was for real. I didn't want to think of Howard right now. It had been so easy to get in. It didn't really make sense. I wanted to think about being a Panther.

And then I remembered.

It couldn't be that! Could it?

I had seen Big Mikey cry, and he had seen me see him. He had asked me to keep it a secret and I had. Was this my reward? Maybe.

I skipped down the road, kicking pebbles. Wait until my parents saw I was a Panther. I bet they'd never seen a real live Panther. They were going to be so happy.

Especially my dad. He wanted me to have a lot of friends. And I did. Eight including Big Mikey. Even though they all had dog names.

I was almost home. The road was getting steeper. I lived on the next block in this big hundred-year-old house on a hill. I wondered if all the other Panthers lived near each other.

I saw a boy from the sixth grade who was riding his bike toward me. "Hey, look, I just got into the Panthers."

The boy stopped and squinted at me under the bright light of the street lamp. He picked up a fold of the sweatshirt between his thumb and forefingers. "Yeah, that's a gray Panther sweatshirt with red and black lettering," he said solemnly. "You steal it?"

I shook my head.

He shrugged and got back on his bike. Over his shoulder he shouted, "Boy, they sure are lowering their standards."

When I got home I snuck back in the same way I'd gotten out, through the basement door. I went up the stairs and walked into the kitchen, pretending to get a snack. My mom and dad were sitting at the kitchen table. They looked up when I came in.

"Scottie, I have good news for you!" my mom said, smiling. I guessed they never knew I was gone.

"I have good news for *you!*" I said.

"You first," my mom said.

My mom is not like a real mom sometimes. I mean she is, but sometimes she acts a little nutty. Like with her part-time job of entering contests. She never really wins anything, though she works awfully hard at it. One time she won one hundred and thirty-five jars of peanut butter. And just my luck. The plain, creamy kind. I was pretty upset until I discovered I could put peanuts in it.

"Well, you'll never believe this in a hundred years, but guess what happened. I was . . ."

My mom couldn't wait.

"Scottie, I won a contest. Look!"

I looked down and there was this pie. First I thought it was a pumpkin pie. Then at closer look I saw it was a peanut butter pie. Not only that, it had this jelly inside. I looked up.

"I won a bake-off contest for my recipe for Jam-butter Pie. A peanut butter and jelly pie. The jelly is Blaustein's Blueberry Jelly. And Scottie, they're coming to take pictures of me and the house and the pies for a women's magazine. I'm famous."

"Not rich, but famous," my father said, smiling.

"Well that's great, Mom," I said, "but listen to this! Tonight—I mean—today I was initiated into a club. The Panthers."

Dad clapped me on the back. "Hey, Scottie, that's just swell."

Both my dad and my mom were grinning from ear to ear. And they just kept grinning. They didn't ask me any questions. Even though what had happened was a secret, I wanted to talk about it a little more. I wished I had a friend not from the Panthers to tell my special news to.

When I lived in Mayfield Heights, friends were no problem. I just had a lot of them. It wouldn't make any sense to call Ralphie, who was my best friend from Mayfield Heights before we moved. We didn't have clubs in my old school, so he probably wouldn't understand. Besides, we didn't really hang out anymore because he lived so far away.

Even though we haven't been living in Chagrin Falls for long, I had a very good friend here, until a few days ago.

One who would understand how very much this meant to me.

But he moved away.

And anyway, he was a ghost.

2
The Ghost Revisited

When I woke up the next morning I thought it had all been a dream. But there on my chair was the sweatshirt. I put it on and looked in the mirror. It was almost unreal; I was now really cool.

When I got on the school bus there were no feet sticking out waiting to trip me. I sat beside my mother's friend's daughter, the spoiled brat, Tracy Deevers. She looked at my sweatshirt, and then did a double take and said nothing. But that was nothing new. Ever since the day our mothers made us play together, and we started to fight, we hadn't had that much to say to each other.

When the bus stopped in the school driveway, I saw Big Mikey heading for the schoolyard.

"Hey, Mikey!" I yelled, running to keep up with him.

He kept walking.

"Yo, Mike?"

11

He turned around and looked at me like he was trying to place the face. That Mikey was sure a scream.

"Listen, Mikey," I said. "I was wondering about this thing . . ."

"Thing?" he said.

"Yeah, you know, like one day no one talks to me, and the next day I get this phone call to be in the coolest club at Jefferson." I didn't add that I'd gotten the feeling last night that the guys were mad at me.

Big Mikey nodded as if he were considering my question.

"I was wondering, though I know how silly this sounds, if maybe you were kind of trying to keep me quiet."

It was hard to say something like that because it made me feel hurt. But it kept rolling around the back of my mind.

"Quiet?" he said.

"Yeah, that's it, you know what I mean."

"Mean?"

Now this was beginning to remind me of my little brother, Brad. Brad is three, and he repeats everything I say. Just the same way Mikey was doing now. It drives me crazy. And my mother has just said she's having another baby. I can't imagine two at home like that.

I also felt as if I was crazy as I explained what I meant to him.

"You know, at the Cleveland Art Museum on

Monday. When we went on that field trip. You got three fingers caught in a mummy's case you were trying to open. And you got scared you would have to stand there for a thousand years or until you died. You thought the other kids had walked ahead. That no one was looking. But I was. And I saw you cry. You were really scared. And you were a real cry baby. And I thought, Could this be the same Big Mikey everyone is afraid of?"

I looked up at Mikey.

He had on a blue, shiny jacket over his Panthers sweatshirt. He was staring down at me. His eyes were almost Day-Glo blue to match his jacket, and his light brown hair stuck out of his head like little spikes. It was really a cool haircut. I wished my mom would let me have one.

As he looked down into my face, I wondered where I had gotten the nerve to speak out like that. It was, of course, all wrong.

When Big Mikey spoke it was in a hoarse whisper. "Yeah, I made you a Panther so you won't tell anyone what happened. I figured I'd do this for you, and then we'd be kind of even."

"So, does this mean I'm not really a Panther?" I hoped he couldn't hear my voice shaking.

"No, listen, you are a Panther. I spared you all those initiation rites. You should be grateful to me, Scott Sheldon. Before I made you one of us, no one knew who you were."

Petey, one of the kids who'd been in the tree-clubhouse, passed by. "Hi, Big Mikey. How ya doin', Stevie?"

I waved back.

"And now you can enjoy all the privileges of being a Panther. You'll be on the best teams in gym. You'll go to the head of the line in the lunchroom. You'll be with the best boys on the playground. You made it."

He started to walk away and then turned around and pointed his finger at me. "Oh, by the way, if you start any nasty rumors, you're automatically out of the Panthers. Think about it. No parties. You'll never be asked to play football. You won't go to the clubhouse meetings. You'll be a nothing again."

I guess I thought it would be easier to pretend the scene in the art museum didn't happen. I hadn't even been a member of the Panthers for one whole day, and I couldn't imagine being the invisible kid again.

"Bye, Mikey," I yelled, running ahead. I didn't want to be late. I wanted everyone to see my sweat-shirt.

When I went to class I kind of pretended nothing was different. But everyone saw. More than a few of the kids stared at me and then turned around and looked again to double-check.

Yeah, it was good to be a Panther. Even if I'd gotten in on a stroke of good luck.

The three Panthers in my class, which was Mrs.

Simon's class, were Petey, Kevin, and Big Mikey. Richie, Blake, Todd, Joey and Jeff were in Mr. Macri's class.

After attendance, Mrs. Simon told us to take out our geography books and turn to the section on the Grand Canyon. I studied it closely. There was something funny in the middle of the canyon. I saw a familiar face waving and smiling.

How could that be? I spaced out. Mrs. Simon's mouth seemed to be moving, but I couldn't hear what she was saying. I must have been imagining things. I got a headache trying to figure it out. It couldn't have been my friend, or ex-friend, the ghost, otherwise known as Malcolm Mallory. But I had eyes! I knew what I saw!

But why would I be daydreaming about a ghost?

I had only just helped him to cross over to the Other Side. He couldn't be anywhere near Ohio. Or the Grand Canyon. He was far, far away where ghosts go to retire.

Malcolm Mallory was the resident ghost of Mallory Manor, which was the same hundred-year-old house that my dad had bought and said was a real deal and my mom had gone crazy fixing up.

It was when I moved into the bedroom my mom had made out of the third-floor attic that I discovered the house was haunted. But the odd thing was my parents couldn't see the ghost. They weren't true believers. My kid brother, Brad, could see him.

And he wasn't telling. Mainly because he doesn't talk much yet.

I looked down at the picture of the Grand Canyon in my textbook. I could swear that was Malcolm himself waving. I knew he was visible on film. You could put him on television or take a picture of him, and he would show up as this old man in old-fashioned clothes. Maybe he was hanging around when they took the snapshot for this book. Malcolm got around, and so did his ghost friends.

"Scottie, do you know the answer to that question?" Mrs. Simon asked.

I almost jumped.

"Hunh?" I said.

"Do you know the answer to the question Tracy just asked?"

I thought about that. I didn't even know the question.

So I said, "No, ma'am, I don't."

The whole class burst out laughing.

Big Mikey nodded his approval. One thing I knew about the Panthers was that they thought it was cool to be kind of dumb in school.

Mrs. Simon said nothing. She just turned to Elise, who knew the answer. I kept waiting for her to say something to me about the way I had acted, but she didn't. It felt good that everyone had laughed. But it also felt bad. My mom wouldn't have liked it.

I tried to pay attention. I like geography. I kept picturing Malcolm. He was on the Other Side, where

I'd helped send him to be with his dear departed wife, Martha. She'd departed in 1900. Even though I knew he was probably really happy, I kind of wished he hadn't left.

We'd had some great times together. Like when we played two-hand touch in my room and his head would substitute itself for the ball. I remembered all the trouble he had gotten me into. One night at dinner he decided to stand right behind me and lift my bowl of soup so it would look as if it were flying in midair.

My parents don't believe in ghosts. Not even at Halloween. So, without thinking, I grabbed the bowl and lifted it to my mouth, drinking down the soup in one gulp.

It was really humiliating. My mom looked at me sadly and said, "What good is a fancy house if your kid's a slob?"

I wondered what Malcolm would think of me being a Panther. All I'd wanted was to have friends. Now everything was okay.

I got the creepy feeling someone was staring at me.

I was right. Howard Fierman's eyes were boring through me like X-ray vision. Mainly he was looking at my Panther sweatshirt as if he couldn't believe it. Well, too bad, I thought. I looked at him. He turned away.

What was I supposed to do—feel guilty? Was it my fault he wasn't asked to be a member of the Panthers? Malcolm would have wanted me to be friends with Howard even though he wasn't popular. It was only right. Howard had been the only person who'd really spoken to me since the first day of school.

Well, if I were to be friends with Howard, everyone—the guys especially—would think I was still a nerd. I was cool now. Howard wasn't cool.

I didn't think too much of Howard, though. I felt special all day. It felt like my birthday, only better. A lot of kids came up to me and talked to me. Most of the time I didn't know what to say. I'd never really spoken to them. The girls, as usual, walked by with their noses stuck in the air. They were really strange that way. They hated the Panthers and all the other boys' clubs.

After school I ran to catch up with the guys.

"Hey, Kevin," I yelled. "Wait up. Wanna play some ball?"

"Not today. I have some stuff to do at home."

"Hey, Joey," I said. "Wanna come over and play with my pinball machine?"

"No. I'm busy."

They ran ahead.

I kicked some pebbles in the school driveway. Might as well get on the school bus and go home. I looked at the leaves falling from trees. Orange, red, yellow, pumpkin. It would be Halloween in about a month.

I sat down quietly in the back of the bus. From the rear window, I got a pretty good view of all the guys going the other way. I felt just as lonely as I had before I was popular. What could they be doing? If they were going to play football, they'd have invited me.

It was confusing. I was a Panther. But I was going home alone again to do my homework alone and play alone. I turned around and saw Howard smiling at me. I turned away.

Before the Panthers, at least I'd had Malcolm to go home to. An invisible friend was better than no friends at all. The problem was no one knew he existed. No one could see him. Maybe he was just a figment of my lonely imagination.

Boy, was I lucky I had people friends now.

I would just have to forget about Malcolm.

Malcolm had probably forgotten about me by now anyway.

Besides, he would never come back.

3

Jam and Jill

When I got home Brad was sitting on the living room floor doing his favorite activity, shredding paper. I looked down just to make sure it wasn't anything of mine. But it was just some old magazines of my mom's. The room looked like a blizzard had hit it.

I said, "Hi, Brad," but it was like he never heard me. He never talked when he was shredding paper. On the other hand, he never talked. I sure hoped for his sake he would start before kindergarten. I wondered if the new little baby would be this way when he was three years old.

I went into the kitchen. My mom was there, talking on the phone.

"Mom?" I said, suddenly smelling something that almost knocked me out.

"Yes, dear, in a minute. Now, Melissa, you can't imagine how shocked I was when I found out."

"Mom?"

"In a minute, dear. Mel, it was like a dream come true."

I guessed she was talking about the new baby

21

she was going to have in about six or seven months. My ears perked up. We had already learned about babies and stuff in school. I knew more than most kids because my dad had told me the facts of life this summer. But he'd left this one out. That you could get babies from eating peanut butter and jelly.

Peanut butter and jelly! That was it!

The whole kitchen smelled like a hot peanut butter and jelly sandwich. My mother walked with her telephone over to the stove, opened the oven, and pulled out not one but five pies.

"Mom?"

"In a minute, dear." She had finished that phone call and dialed someone else. "Lisa, I am so excited. Just imagine, *Women's Circle* is coming to my home. Oh, yes, I've been cleaning ever since I heard. The house is spotless."

I thought of the blizzard in the living room.

"I got a dress for the photo session. It's pink. I think it goes with the peanut butter and jelly pies. They just might include the recipe on the top of Blaustein's Blueberry Jelly jars. Also . . ."

"Mom?"

"What *is* it, Scottie?"

I stared at her.

I forgot. But I knew it was something.

"Nothing," I said.

She looked at me oddly.

I ran up the stairs two at a time to do my homework.

On a rack in the corner was my collection of hats. I had a silver hat with wings. It made me want to run. A fireman's hat, which was bright red and said Mayfield Heights Fire Department, and my cowboy hat, which slipped down over my ears. I put on my blue baseball hat with Cleveland Indians on it and turned it sideways. Then I sharpened my pencils for a real long time in my electric pencil sharpener my grandma bought me for Christmas.

I began to read my geography book. My eyes stared at the words, but I couldn't seem to concentrate. If my mom hadn't called up that there was a phone call for me, I would have fallen asleep. I skipped down the steps. I wondered who it was— Blake, Kevin, Richie, Todd. I could do my homework later if there was a football game or something. Maybe they'd want to come over here and meet my mom. Well, if she could tear herself away from the phone.

"Hi!" I said happily into the phone. I knew someone would finally call. "Joe's Bar and Grill."

"Very funny joke," came the sarcastic reply.

I sank down cross-legged on the floor. What a disappointment.

"Oh, hi, Howard."

"Hi, Scottie. I was wondering if you wanted to come and do your geography homework with me. It's really hard tonight."

"I can't. I have some kids coming over," I lied. There was an awkward pause.

"Well, I won't bother you anymore, Scottie. If that's how it is. You are sure lucky to be in that club."

I was waiting for him to say "How did it happen?" But he didn't. To him, I'd been popular already. I stood up, said goodbye, and hung up the phone.

I also felt lousy.

Howard always made me feel so guilty. It wasn't fair. I wasn't going to stop being nice to him just because I was a Panther. But I didn't have to play with him after school or eat my lunch with him, either.

I felt hungry. Whenever I'm unhappy I eat. My mom says my stomach's like a bottomless pit because I can eat and eat and eat and never feel full. I never gain any weight, either.

I looked in the kitchen. Now there were eight pies lined up.

"What's that, Linda?" my mom was asking the phone. "Make them in different sizes and shapes? Yes, I could do that."

"Mom?"

"Not now, dear. But Linnie, that wouldn't be hard! Oh, that's great. Of course you can have the recipe."

I looked at the pies. They were high and thick. I leaned down to smell one and came up with peanut butter on my nose. Oozy, drooly, piping hot peanut butter was inside the pie, and hot, blueberry jelly bubbled down the sides.

I'd never seen anything like it. For a second I

thought I'd faint. A hot, giant peanut butter and jelly pie. These pies were a dream come true.

Suddenly all I could think of was a gigantic glass of cold milk.

Finally my mother got off the phone.

"Scottie, did you want to ask me something?"

"I, uh, yeah, Mom, something's come up."

The phone rang again.

We both looked at it.

"Give me a sec, Skeeter-Scooter, and then I'm all yours."

It wasn't that I wanted to tell her something, really. It's just that something was bothering me, and I wanted to talk. But I wanted her to pull it out of me. She was good at that.

Except now she was busy. She had never won a really big contest, and it was taking up all her time.

I got her attention and pointed to the pie. She smiled and nodded, only she went right on talking. I took a knife and cut a big wedge. Then I went to the refrigerator, took out the milk, and poured myself a big, cold glass.

"What do I call it, Susan? Oh, Jill's Jambutter Pie."

I sat down, tucked a napkin in my shirt so I wouldn't get my sweatshirt dirty, picked up my fork, and dug in. The taste went way beyond a peanut butter and jelly sandwich, which was my favorite lunch. It was more like a huge, hot, yummy cookie. But it was a pie.

"How do you like it, Scottie?" my mother asked.

"Oh, *goo er eh genuth,*" I said, nodding my head furiously.

I mean peanut butter and jelly does stick to the roof of your mouth, any way you eat it.

"Susie, my son loves it. Maybe I'll be famous. Maybe the commercials for Blaustein's Blueberry Jelly will star Scottie."

Wow, I always wanted to be on television. Maybe I could wear my Panthers sweatshirt.

At first I didn't hear it over my mom's voice. There was a back door off the kitchen, and someone was knocking on it. It got up to see who it was. It was kind of late for the paper boy, who usually came to the front door anyway.

My mouth was still full of peanut butter and jelly, but I managed to say, "Hi, guys."

There were five Panthers. I guessed they'd come to play. The only ones missing were Kevin, Richie, and Big Mikey.

"Hey, I'm glad you came over," I said, trying not to sound too thrilled. "Listen there's a horse in the barn if any of you want to ride. We just got him. Or there's the duck pond. We could play around there. Or you can come in, 'cause my mom just baked these peanut butter and jelly pies.

"Come outside so we can talk," Todd said.

My heart sank. Did they want to kick me out of the club already?

"My mom doesn't care. She's been on the phone for hours. You can come in."

"No," Blake said, "It's safer to be secret. That's why we always knock on the back door."

Suddenly I felt strange. I wasn't sure if it was because I ate all that pie too fast or because I might be asked to do something I couldn't. Then what would I do?

I stepped into the backyard with the guys.

"The thing is, Scottie," Joey said, "we're having a party."

"Gosh, that's great. What should I bring? I could bring a pie. See, it's made out of peanut butter and jelly and . . ."

Blake cut me off. "Chill out, Scottie. We don't have parties like other kids do. This isn't a birthday party, got it?"

All the guys nodded. I felt stupid.

"Okay. Well, where is it?"

"Well, that's a secret," Petey said, "but you'll be notified. It's after school tomorrow. Tell your mom you'll be a little late."

"Sounds great," I said.

I was getting to be good at keeping secrets lately. First I had to pretend I wasn't best friends with a ghost, then I had to make it look to my parents like I was this well-adjusted kid. That was before I got into the Panthers. Now that I was in I had to keep a secret party secret. If things kept going this way, I was going to grow up to be a great CIA or FBI agent.

As I went back inside, pie number nine was coming out of the oven, and my mother was still talking on the phone. The telephone cord was wrapped around her like a snake.

"Nancy, it's just too exciting. And such a plus for the community of Chagrin Falls. Why, yes, I would love to speak at your bridge club meeting on entering and winning contests. Oh, yes, I'll bring some pies. What's another batch?"

When she hung up I said, "You sure have a lot of friends."

"Well, I work at it. Just like you did, Skeeter-Scooter. We're very proud of you. Your father and I were worried about you once. Now, what did you want to talk about?"

I thought for a moment. I opened my mouth, and the phone rang.

She smiled at me. I shrugged. "I guess it can wait, Mom."

Then I thought of how far I'd come. I had been *almost* a kid with problems. Invisible. But now I was a Panther.

I thought again about the visit from the Panthers minus Kevin, Richie, and Big Mikey. It couldn't have been that they were playing ball or anything, because then there would have been seven guys plus Big Mikey. They couldn't have been playing before they came over, could they? Still, they did drop by to invite me to a party. They did come all the way over to my house.

As I went into the living room, I thought maybe it took a little longer to really be included in the group. Then I went back to thinking about the party. I wondered what it would be like.

"Hi, Scottie." My dad was home. He hung up his hat in the big hall closet and put his briefcase away.

"Hi, Dad."

"How are my two boys?" he asked, looking around at Brad's mess.

I said, "Great, Dad. I'm going to a party after school tomorrow." I didn't say who was giving it.

Brad sat in a pool of shredded paper and said, smiling eagerly, ". . . tomorrow."

I hated when he did that. Which was always.

And he always stared at me, smiling, like he liked me a lot.

"Scott, I'm glad you've made friends. We were frankly, your mother and I, just a little concerned about you. Especially when you saw ghosts."

Brad began to jump up and down on top of his mountain of paper balls and strips. He gets away with murder. If I ever made a mess like that in the living room, my mom would kill me.

He fell down and, feet straight in the air, yelled, ". . . ghost." And then he giggled.

My dad gave me a look that said, now look what you've done.

"He just likes to repeat words, Dad," I said. But I looked at Brad the Brat, who was starting to turn a somersault on his paper pile. He liked to repeat my words. He had said "ghost," and it wasn't me who had said the word. It was my dad. Only my dad didn't look at it that way.

I wondered what was going on in my brother's tricky little brain, even though I wasn't sure he had one yet. Was he just making trouble, or was trouble on its way?

4
The Secret Party

The next morning I rubbed my eyes and looked out over the rooftops from my attic window. Prince II, who slept under my bed, ran out, looked around, and sniffed. It was cold out.

I leaped out of bed and got dressed, putting on a turtleneck jersey under my Panthers sweatshirt. Today was a special Friday. It was the day of the secret party.

I wondered how and when they would tell me when and where it was.

I charged down the steps and into the kitchen. My mom was talking on the phone. Brad was mushing his cereal with his spoon. A typical morning at the Sheldon home—except for the smell. Very sweet and very strong. I glanced over at the kitchen counter and then quickly looked again. There must have been about twenty more pies. I even could see two on top of the refrigerator.

I got a bowl, poured in my favorite cereal, and drowned it in milk. My stomach growled. I suddenly wasn't very hungry. I was going to put sugar in my cereal, but it didn't seem to need it.

My mom hung up, looked at me, and said, "Don't you have something else to wear, dear? You wore that last night. There're clean clothes in the basket in the basement."

"Mom, this is my club sweatshirt."

"I know. But you don't have to wear it all the time. I wonder what the other mothers say?"

I thought about that. I didn't know who the other mothers were. I didn't really even know their sons.

The phone rang again. I was getting tired of all my mother's friends. Wait until they came over, and Brad found their pocketbooks and dumped them upside down all over the floor.

"Carol," my mother was saying. "You must come over for lunch. Well, of course, coffee and pie for dessert. Yes, I'd like that."

A little peanut butter and jelly went a long way, I figured. Maybe I should bring a pie to the Panthers' secret party after all.

Later, after we piled out of the school bus, I ran across the yard and caught up to Richie. "Where's the party? Do you know yet?"

He gave me a dirty look. "Shh, do you want everyone to come?"

"No, of course not. But how will I know where to go?"

"You'll be told," he said, and ran ahead.

That morning I waited and waited, but none of the guys said anything. What if they forgot? What if they whispered it so low that I missed it?

Suddenly I heard Mrs. Simon yell, "Scott, Scott Sheldon. Are you with us?"

"No, Mrs. Simon," I said.

Oh my gosh! How could I say that?

The whole class laughed. But I earned the Panther Seal of Approval from Big Mikey. He shot a rubber band from the tip of his pencil, and it hit the tip of my ear.

I had no trouble hearing what Mrs. Simon said next. "Scott, I think you should plan to spend some time with me after school today."

After school? No way, not today! What about the secret party?

Then a hand passed me a note written on lined paper and folded to about the size of a dime.

I opened it up.

It was from Kevin. It said, "Eetmay emay in the ardyay after oolschay."

How could I do that now? I had to stay after school with Mrs. Simon.

I caught up with Kevin in the hall. Before I could say anything he said simply, "We'll wait for you."

That made me feel wonderful all afternoon. Until after school. When I went into Mrs. Simon's room she wasn't there, but she'd written on the blackboard: DON'T GO AWAY, SCOTT SHELDON. I'M WITH THE PRINCIPAL.

Now I didn't feel so great. How long would she be? How long would the guys wait? I wondered if she was talking to the principal about me.

I began to feel very nervous. I wished she'd hurry up and come back and we could get it over with.

Finally I heard the click of her heels.

"Okay, Scottie," she said. "I'm not going to keep you after school forever . . ."

Well, that was a relief. Only I needed to be dismissed in about the next ten minutes.

"I just wanted to tell you how happy I am to be your teacher and that you're a very good student and a gifted boy. I just wonder why you chose to let us all down by pretending you don't have a brain. Is that your idea of being one of the guys, Scottie?"

"Hunh?"

"Scottie, I can read sweatshirts. I see a gray sweatshirt with black and red lettering and a menacing panther on it. Fine. Wear whatever you want. But does wearing that particular sweatshirt mean you can't have manners? Because one day you'll grow and be too big for that sweatshirt, and you'll be stuck with being a real dummy."

"Uh-huh."

"What are we going to do about this, Scott?"

"Um, well, I'm going to try harder to do good in school, Mrs. Simon."

"Do well, Scottie. That is correct grammar."

I looked at the desk, and then I looked up. She was smiling at me.

"I believe you can pull yourself out of this slump, Scottie. Don't let me down."

I shook my head and ran out of the room and into the hall and reached the yard. I had no trouble finding the Panthers. Of all the groups in the yard, they were the noisiest.

As I ran toward them, I looked across the yard and saw Tracy Deevers and a gang of girls. They had a club called the Pussycats, and they wore these hot pink satin jackets with embroidered kittens on them. I heard that all of the girls in that club had to buy their own jackets.

One of the girls stuck out her tongue and blew a raspberry at me.

"Oh, give yourself a fur ball," Petey shouted.

"BOYS, BOYS, THEY'RE NO GOOD. THEY ALWAYS THINK THEY'RE IN HOLLYWOOD!" they chanted. Tracy and her club of about ten girls shouted until their faces began to match the color of their jackets.

The Panthers came back with their chant, "GIRLS, GIRLS, GO AWAY. COME BACK AGAIN SOME OTHER DAY!" I yelled it louder than the others. It wasn't tops for originality, but it did the trick. The girls walked away and began waiting for the school bus with some of the other kids who didn't belong to a club.

That's when I saw him coming across the yard. Like a moving target. I almost wanted to wave him away. I stuck my head inside my sweatshirt. I knew what was coming.

Howard Fierman walked across the yard, and the Panthers yelled, "PICK, HOWARD, PICK." He began to run toward the bus stop. The chanting got louder, "PICK, HOWARD, PICK."

As he passed me, I looked away, but I could see the dirty look he shot me. Instead of feeling bad, though, I got angry. How many times had I told him to take his fingers out of his nose? In a way it was his own fault.

We watched the school bus leave.

Everyone looked up at Big Mikey. I understood that only he knew where the Panthers' secret party was.

"It's at my house," he said. Everyone nodded as if they knew it would be there.

"Did anyone buy the chips and soda pop?" Richie said.

"The new boy should," Kevin said.

Everyone nodded. Big Mikey gave me some money, and they all started to walk away.

"Hey, wait up," I yelled. They all turned.

"Mikey, where do you live?"

He pointed. "Two blocks over that way. On Cedar Street." Then he pointed in the opposite direction. "But the store is about five and a half blocks down on West Broadway. Got it?"

I walked and I walked until I found a little grocery on the corner. It was more like seven and a half blocks. I stood for ten minutes deciding which chips they would want. I finally went for the basic brands—boring, but safe.

Before I left the store, I saw it was close to four-thirty. I had to be home by six. And I didn't have my bike.

I ran all the way back to Big Mikey's house. Well, almost all the way. Even down the street before I got there I heard rock music blaring. When I walked in, the party was in full swing. Richie had a real ciga-rette in his hand. He wasn't smoking it or anything. He just held it in his palm.

"What's happening?" I screamed at Blake, bringing the potato chips and the cans of cola into the living room.

"Happening?"

"What kinds of games are you playing?"

"Playing?"

I sighed. Either it was the really loud music, or everyone seemed to talk like Brad again. Then Big Mikey came toward me. He leaned over and said, smiling, "Say, Scottie, would you mind running down to the gas station on the corner and getting some ice. The drinks are hot, and we're all out."

I looked around the room. Everyone was star-ing at me. Then I looked at the clock. Five-ten. I ran to the corner, picked up the ice, and ran back with the bag knocking against my knees until they felt cold.

Inside, the party was still jumping. Two guys

were dancing, imitating a girl and a guy. One had a lamp shade on his head. Kevin was standing on his head with a banana in his mouth, and he was eating it. Some of the guys were on the phone. They were making phonies.

"Hi, is Roger there?"

"No one by the name of Roger lives here."

There were peals of laughter as the guys rolled around the carpet. No one by the name of Roger lived there.

Then Richie dialed the same number again, the cigarette still in the palm of his hand.

"Hi, is Roger there?"

He did that about five times. I wondered why the other person picked up the phone. Even from where I sat I heard this loud scream, "Leave me alone, you little brat."

Then came the last call. I never saw anyone do this right, not even my friends in my old neighborhood.

Richie dialed one more time, an easy smile on his face, and said coolly, "Hi, this is Roger. Any messages?"

The guys collapsed in laughter, rolling over on the carpet and punching at each other with their fists. I had tears rolling down my eyes. And when I laugh that hard, I can't catch my breath and I get the hiccups.

So this was what a Panthers party was like. It

was great. Gosh, I was glad to be a part of it, even though I missed half of it getting stuff.

Big Mikey looked around the room. "Uh-oh, it's a mess. My mom will have my head. We'd better clean up." Everyone looked around. Then everyone looked at me.

"He should clean up. He's the new guy."

No one said anything.

I didn't know what to say. If I cleaned very fast and then ran at top speed, I could make it home by six-fifteen. Fifteen minutes late wasn't so bad.

The guys left for a quick game of touch football while I got to work. I picked up the empty cans and threw away all the garbage I saw. I moved a few chairs and tables back to what I thought were their original positions. I even straightened out the pillows on the sofa.

Then I saw it. A whole bag of potato chips had spilled onto the carpet, and when the guys were rolling around laughing, they'd ground them in.

I sat down with a plop on one of the couches. It wasn't fair. I wanted to be out playing touch football. I didn't join a club to be a maid. If I had gone through the whole initiation, maybe the guys would include me more. But Big Mikey insisted I be in, and didn't that make me just as much a part of the group?

It was just so confusing to be in. I was a part of everything, but I didn't know if they really liked me.

Even though it had been awful, life sure had been a lot easier before I'd become a Panther.

I was looking around for a vacuum when this really short woman came in carrying three bags of groceries.

"Hi. How are you? I'm Mikey's ma," she said. "Are you a Panther? From the looks of things, you must have had one of your silly parties."

I just stared at her. She was really short, and Mikey was so big and tall. I couldn't believe it.

"Oh, I know. You're the new boy Mikey told me about. Here, let me help you clean up. How was the party?"

"Oh," I said, "We laughed a lot. It was a good party."

"And then they stuck you with the cleanup," Mikey's mom said. "Aren't you the little boy whose mother won that contest?"

I nodded.

"I'd just love to make that peanut butter and jelly pie. Could you ask your mother for the recipe?"

"Sure."

She got out the vacuum cleaner, and I looked at my watch. I had to run really fast to get home. Big Mikey came back in with Jeff and Petey. Petey clamped me on the shoulder. Jeff asked me how I was doing. I began to feel more like one of the guys.

I said goodbye and ran out the door.

Well, I was one of the guys. I was a Panther. It sure was better than being a nobody, I decided.

5
Peanut Butter and Jelly Nightmare

"Mom, I'm home," I said when I got in. No answer. She must be on the phone upstairs.

I took a deep whiff and shut my eyes. The whole house smelled like a hot peanut butter and jelly sandwich. The air seemed heavy.

Prince II was sleeping by the fireplace in the living room, snoring. Brad was walking around, eyes open, crashing into things like he was in a daze. I walked into the kitchen. All I could think of was milk. An ice cold glass of milk.

Just then I heard my dad's voice. "I'm home, dear."

My mom came downstairs and kissed him. "Jack."

He smiled. "Jill."

I looked at the ceiling. I hated it when they started that mushy Jack and Jill stuff.

"Baking again, dear?" he asked.

41

That was the understatement of the year.

"Scottie," my mother said to me suddenly. "You and Brad set the table in the dining room, please. I want to talk to your father."

Brad staggered into the dining room carrying three wooden salad bowls, and I brought in all the rest of the stuff. Actually, what my mother said had sounded bad, now that I thought about it. Whenever she said she wanted to talk to my father, I was usually in trouble.

Finally we all sat down in the dining room.

"Your mother wants me to talk to you, Scottie." My mom looked down.

"Could you pass the peanut butter and jelly?" I said. "I mean, can I have some peas and carrots?"

That smell was everywhere. I marveled at how roast beef and peas and carrots could smell like a hot peanut butter and jelly sandwich.

My dad checked the time on his watch, and then he loosened the collar of his shirt. "Scottie, I have something to say to you."

My mother was busy cutting Brad's roast beef into tiny little pieces.

"Your mother went to school today."

Uh-oh. Mrs. Simon. She sure didn't waste any time.

"Do you want to know what I saw, Scottie?" She saw us making fun of Howard Fierman in the yard. Or the girls.

"I saw you playing with your friends after

school, and I saw that Tracy Deevers was crying. In fact, Mrs. Deevers called me up to say that the boys were out of hand."

"Why did you go to school?" I asked softly.

"I had to prepare for a PTA meeting. They asked me to bake some pies."

I decided to like Mrs. Simon again.

Then my dad said, "Now, you know how much we want you to have friends and be in this club. And we know how much you've tried. But try a little harder to be a good boy. We don't want you to have problems with girls when you grow up."

I nodded.

After dinner I went up to my room. It's a good thing I have such a great room, because I seem to spend a lot of time in it. When we moved in, my mom put in a pinball machine that worked and a big bookshelf for all my games and books. My favorite thing is sitting on my knees and looking out the window over the roof to the treetops. I can see our duckless duck pond and the stable where my dad keeps our new horse, which is okay as long as I don't have to ride it. I couldn't wait to have the guys over to see my room. We could have a lot of fun up here.

The smell had followed me upstairs.

Even though I'd had a big piece of pie for dessert, I just had to have another slice. Was it the aroma, or was I unhappy? I don't usually eat *this* much without a reason. But I wasn't that unhappy. After all, I was a Panther now.

I went down to the kitchen and helped myself to another big slice. When I got back up to my room I felt suddenly strange. Little green spots started to jump around in front of my eyes. Maybe this time I had eaten too much. I got undressed, crawled into my bed, and tried to fall asleep.

But I felt even more dizzy and sick. For a minute I thought I would break my record and throw up all over the floor. Then I realized—I wasn't sick that way. Suddenly Prince II ran under my bed.

The room had turned a sickly shade of Day-Glo green.

"Oooh noooo," I moaned.

"Oooh yeeees," came a shimmery voice. It sounded like it was coming from underwater.

It sounded like . . . but it couldn't be her . . . or it!

Just then a flash of hot pink light lit up the room, and then faded like a firecracker. A beautiful purple cat sat in the middle of the floor.

Prince II crawled out from under the bed and growled.

"Napatha?" I asked in a small voice.

"None other," said the talking purple cat. Her voice was a soft purr. Her fur was a vivid lavender.

Napatha was a ghost friend of my friend the ghost, Malcolm. She could change herself into anything she wanted to be. Mostly she swam around at the Taj Mahal like a mermaid.

"Wow, I'm sure happy to see you, Napatha," I

squealed. "I haven't seen a real live ghost in a while. Say, how's Malcolm? And how's his wife, Martha? Any news from the Other Side?"

Without answering she shimmered and hissed and arched her purple back. She fizzed out like a light that burns out. The room wasn't green anymore. It was just my room, and outside was the inky black night. It was late. I yawned. Well, maybe it was a dream after all.

I tucked myself in.

That's when I heard the crackle of lightning. I jumped up in bed and looked out the window. It wasn't raining. Could the lightning have been in my room?

Then the room was instantly hot green, hot blue, hot red, and sizzling orange. Not to mention the bright white lightning that kept flashing on and off. Where was Napatha? I was beginning to get very, very scared.

"Napatha?"

There was no answer.

I gulped.

There was a new you-know-what in the room!

6
The Ghastly Ghost

Suddenly the floor began to rock like a ride in an amusement park. The wooden floorboards seemed to come together, separate, then come together again. My bed was like a boat in rocky waters. I clutched the sides, terrified. I mean, it isn't every kid who gets stuck in a horror movie.

I held my breath. Was it Malcolm? Was Malcolm coming back? But that was impossible! He'd just left.

It must be a new ghost. There must be a bunch of them that haunted this old house. Maybe another house was here before this one. Maybe this ghost was from the Revolutionary War. Why did my parents have to move? I didn't need this kind of excitement.

There was a flash of light, and I saw a shadow wavering on the wall. If that was the ghost, he was tall and thin. Very tall. The light went off, and the ghost vanished in the darkness.

Just then all my books started flying around the

room like there was a hurricane. Then my games flew lower. It was awful! This new ghost was a real slob.

I began to get angry. I'd had it with ghosts. Nothing could scare me. Or almost nothing.

I watched as all my books and games flew back to the bookshelves. Whoever this new ghost was, he sure was putting on some super show.

There was a low moan. The moan got louder, and everything started to shake again. Prince II leaped on top of my bed. Soon we were shaking so much, my teeth were chattering and his fur was standing straight up.

I heard another moan.

Then I heard someone—something—laugh. And I knew it wasn't me. I had nothing to laugh about. This was Ghost City.

I drew in my breath sharply. I was terrified!

On the wall was a hooded ghost about ten feet tall with sunken eyes and long, knobby hands. I knew a little something about ghosts and their tricks, but that didn't help. I wanted to run away, but I was afraid the ghost would catch me.

"Who is it?" I whispered desperately. Like it would be better if the ghost had a name.

I closed my eyes and whistled to calm my nerves. It didn't help. I waited for the new trick feeling I'd thought of, pretending I was alone in a time machine.

Then came a groan that sounded like a roar.

"Hello?" I yelled. "Hello there."

There was a clank of chains. Only this time they didn't drop. Malcolm had always dropped his chains. Usually he hit his foot.

Next the clanking was replaced by a voice. A loud, frightening voice that belonged to the ten-foot ghost in white robes with hollow, sunken eyes whose shadow or picture was still on my wall.

As Prince II and I began to shake again, I wondered how life would be with a mean ghost. A real serious, spooky ghost who wouldn't play two-hand touch. Suddenly I began to miss Malcolm.

Then I heard, "Scottttiiieee . . ."

My mouth fell open. I couldn't answer that.

Then I heard, "Sco . . . Sco . . . Sco . . ." It sounded scratchy. Like a record player that was stuck in one spot. I quickly reached over and switched on my clown lamp.

Then I knew. There was no tall, professional ghost on that wall. I got up and looked at my record player. No one was yelling Scottie. There was a record on it called "Sound Effects for Ghosts."

I had been tricked. By a ghost.

"Malcolm?" I asked softly.

"None other," came a voice. "Long time no see, my boy."

"Malcolm, where are you?"

"Well, my boy, I'm not quite sure yet."

How could that be? He was the ghost I'd just sent to the Other Side, a retiring place for ghosts.

And now he was back? He had been gone less than a week.

"Can you give me any clues?" I asked.

"Well, dear boy, I'm back from the Other Side. But I'm not quite sure I'm fully on This Side, if you know what I mean," the quivering voice said.

"But, why, Malcolm? Why did you come back? It took so much trouble to get you there. Remember? We had to find a windmill that hadn't been there for a hundred years. Then we had to concentrate and concentrate, and suddenly you were gone. We could never do that again, Malcolm. I hope you like Chagrin Falls, Ohio."

The windmill was why Malcolm had trouble materializing. When he was alive, he was inside the windmill. That's when the fatal accident happened. He ate a banana and then tossed the peel. When he got up to leave he tripped on it, slid across the windmill floor, and fell out the window. He got sliced into parts on his way down. That's why he always had trouble collecting himself. I met Malcolm because he came back home to haunt Martha, his wife, who died in 1900. He just never really left.

Suddenly a head flew across the room and landed on or in the globe on my desk. It was Malcolm's head all right, with his fringy, white hair and half-balding globe. One of his eyes was where Africa should be.

"Just getting myself together, dear boy. Oh,

dear, a rainstorm must be on the way. All my parts are rusty."

"But, Malcolm, why the Super Special Show? Why didn't you just materialize? Or try to materialize?"

Just then Prince II began to purr and then growl. He was up on his haunches. Prince II never much liked ghosts.

"Hey, Malcolm, are you okay?" I shouted. He was nowhere to be seen.

"I've lost my powers, Scottie, my boy."

"No, you haven't, Malcolm. Keep trying. Remember to concentrate!"

In seconds he was almost fully materialized, and I clapped my hands together. "Nearly there, Malcolm, but not quite," I said. "Now, if you can just put your arm where your leg is supposed to be, take your nose off your forehead, and then turn your head around to face the front, I think you might just about look right."

There was a display of bright lights.

"Whoops!" he said.

And then the light faded, and there was Malcolm in his longish jacket, striped pants, and a vest with a watch on a chain. He always looked like a walking costume party.

"Nice show, Malcolm," I said.

He laughed and laughed. And when Malcolm laughs his stomach shakes like a bowl of Jell-O.

"Did I scare you?" he asked.

"I'm scared that you're back. What made you do it, Malcolm?"

He wasn't talking.

"And why didn't you just show up?"

"Scottie, my dear boy. Ghosts don't show up without showing off. I owe it to my ghost ego. Of course, it was Napatha's idea. She's such a spook."

"Did Nappy come over to the Other Side?"

"That she did, my boy. And she turned the Other Side upside down, I'll tell you that much."

Prince II was walking backward. I patted him on the head and so did Malcolm, saying, "Prince the Second, is it?"

"I'm in the Panthers now, Malcolm," I announced. "It's the most popular boys' club in Jefferson Grammar School."

Malcolm nodded, and I thought for sure his head would roll off.

"I have a sweatshirt and everything. Remember when I didn't have any friends at all?"

"I know all about it, Scottie. In fact, that's why I'm back."

"But how did you know, if you were on the Other Side, somewhere over the rainbow?"

"Well, we ghosts have our ways."

"So you know how much fun I'm having?" I asked, testing him.

"Oh, my, my, loads of fun. But I also know how you got into that club. You can thank your lucky stars that Oversized Mikey got his three big fingers caught in that mummy's case."

"I'm so glad you're back, Malcolm." It was great having someone I could really talk to again.

"You were over on the Other Side about four days, Mal. What must Martha think?" When I got close to this ghost, I started to talk like him.

"Oh, no, we measure time differently over there. Actually, I stayed for several hundred years. Martha's rather fond of you. She thinks of you like a grandson to us."

"Wanna play?" I asked my friend.

Malcolm and I began to play two-hand touch football using his head as a ball. I laughed as Malcolm, who was transparent, went right through the pinball machine and passed through me.

I had forgotten how solid friendship could be.

Malcolm was a true friend.

I was sure I could never be angry with him.

7

Peanut Butter and Jelly Saturday

The next morning I woke up to a small but strange thing gliding into the room. It was Brad with his blanket over his head. There was a bump near the top where he was sucking his thumb.

"Ghost," he said.

"Go away, Brad," I said, sleepily. "There are no ghosts. Don't talk like that. Mommy will get angry."

I wondered if Malcolm was back for good or had just popped in for a quick visit. Brad said "ghost" again, like it was his favorite word, and then glided out of the room. I heard him trip on the first step.

Then I saw Malcolm. He was still here! He was hanging upside down from a curtain rod.

It was raining outside.

Malcolm said, "A pouring, boring Saturday. This old house is noted for those."

"It might not be so bad," I said.

In midconversation I saw my mom at the door. She had about a dozen pink hair rollers in her hair.

"I thought I heard you talking to someone. Who was that?"

"Brad came into my room, Mom. I was talking to him. He just left. And then I turned the radio on for a few seconds," I said.

"And you were nice to him?" she asked. I thought she was going to cry. Whenever I was actually nice to Brad, she started to cry.

Then I remembered why my mother was acting so funny. This wouldn't be a pouring, boring Saturday. This was the day the blueberry jelly people were coming. Wow! I jumped out of bed.

"Today's my big day, Scottie. Will you do me a favor and mind the baby so he doesn't get overexcited?"

Overexcited? Brad's favorite game was finding a full pocketbook and dumping everything out of it. And sometimes he hid some of the things.

Cute.

"Now, Scottie, I want you to wear your new navy blazer and a white shirt. Put on your gray flannel pants, the ones with the cuffs. And wear your new red tie."

"Can't I wear my sweatshirt?" I thought the jelly people would be impressed. I was about to say so, but my mother shot me a look that said the sweatshirt was forbidden. No discussion.

When my mother left the room, Malcolm said,

"What is that delightful fragrance she had on?" He'd come down off the curtains and was sitting in or on the pinball machine.

"Oh, the smell? That's the peanut butter and jelly pies she bakes. It gets to you."

It was painful putting on dress-up clothes on a Saturday. After I finally tied the tie, Malcolm and I went down the steps. Malcolm was in a frisky mood. He went down head first, walking on his hands, his feet in the air. I wondered if he could keep his head on.

Then I looked at his mouth. It looked upside down. With some effort, he said, "This ought to amuse Bradley. Keep him out of trouble."

By the time we reached the bottom Brad was laughing so hard he was hiccuping. My mom had to slap him on the back.

"Well, Brad is certainly excited about my big day," my mom said.

I didn't want to tell her the real reason why Brad was so excited. It seemed like Malcolm wanted to take over my job of keeping Brad entertained. This could be one of those days when there was no stopping Malcolm. I wondered if he might ruin his mission trying so hard. Of course, I couldn't say anything. If I could, whom would I tell?

My mom made us some cereal which tasted, of course, like peanut butter and jelly. I never wanted a peanut butter and jelly sandwich again.

I counted the pies. I knew my mom had baked

a lot for the photographers, but it seemed like one was missing. After my second count I saw it was on top of the refrigerator. I counted a third time. Then I looked up.

Malcolm had eaten a piece of pie à la mode— which means it had a scoop of ice cream on it. Sometimes he would come in and have a banana or some cookies or a piece of carrot cake. The weird thing was even though Malcolm was invisible, what he ate wasn't. It would land in his stomach whole. I felt like I had X-ray vision. I saw eight slices of pie and lots of ice cream in Malcolm's tummy. Or eight slices of peanut butter and jelly pie and ice cream floating in midair. Talk about science fiction.

I stood in front of him nervously. I had left my cereal practically uneaten on the kitchen table. Brad was sucking on his spoon, watching.

"Anything wrong, Skeeter?"

I hate it when my mom starts with those nicknames. Maybe next year, when I graduate from elementary school, she'll stop.

"Why, wrong? Wrong? Everything's right," I said. I wished the food in Malcolm's stomach would turn invisible. Brad was still sucking on his spoon, only now he was making sounds.

"Are you nervous about today, Scooter-pie?"

"Yes, Mom, you bet I am," I said. My imagination wasn't advanced enough to think up the kinds of pranks Malcolm could play because he decided to take care of Brad today.

Brad.

I looked around.

He wasn't sitting at the table. Where'd he gone? We looked all over the house, but he wasn't anywhere.

Finally I yelled, "I found him, Mom."

Brad was outside with no jacket, helping the men in the van unload the cameras and other stuff they needed. My mom took one look out the window, and then ran upstairs to get dressed.

I was stuck getting Brad.

"C'mon, Brad, you'll only get in everyone's way," I said, helping him on with his jacket.

". . . way," he repeated.

"Are you Mrs. Sheldon's little boy?" said this lady, looking down at me and smiling. She was carrying a clipboard. "Aren't you cute."

Of course, she meant Brad. I wouldn't wait for him to get to her pocketbook.

"My name is Scott Sheldon," I said. Then as an afterthought I added, "This is my little brother, Brad. He's only three."

"Isn't he adorable," she said.

I ran upstairs to get my mother. I was halfway up the steps when I heard her scream, "Oh, no!"

I raced up the steps two at a time. I hadn't had a glimpse of Malcolm in a long time. But when I got up to the bedroom, I saw it was just my mother's nerves. Her new necklace had broken, and the pearls were rolling across the floor.

"Pick something else, Mom. Here," I said, and handed her a big pin made out of pearls.

Just then Brad was at the door. "Here! People here! Come, Mommy. Now!"

My mother clasped her hands together. "He's talking. We should do this more often."

Before going down, she paused at the top of the steps. She took my hand and squeezed it. "Oh, Scottie, I'm scared to death."

"Mom," I said. "You'll be great. You won the contest. You invented those peanut butter and jelly pies. You bought a bright pink dress to wear. Now go down there and be a star!"

She held my hand even harder. Then she looked around.

"Where's Brad?"

"Brad? He was just here, wasn't he? He must be downstairs."

"With the magazine people by himself!"

Then we both yelled together. "Brad's in there alone!" And we ran down the stairs.

It sure did wonders for my mom's stage fright.

Brad was sitting on the coffee table waving his little legs, taking apart one of the cameras like it was a jigsaw puzzle. My mother grabbed it. He held on to it fiercely, but she got it and in a very high, squeaky voice said to everyone, "Hi. My name is Jill Sheldon."

"Mrs. Sheldon," said the lady with the clipboard I had met outside, "I can't tell you how thrilled

we are to have you in our magazine. All of our readers will be charmed. My, what a delightful house.
And to think you made all those marvelous cre-
ations, those superb peanut and jelly pies right here
in your kitchen. Where is your lovely kitchen, Mrs.
Sheldon?"

She said all that in one breath.

We walked into the kitchen.

"Oh, what fabulous linoleum." My mom and I
looked down. "We should have some shots of you in
your kitchen, which must be the nerve center of this
absolutely charming home."

I looked up at my mom. I wondered if she'd
ever get a chance to say something.

"Well, I for one would like a cup of your marvelous coffee, Mrs. Sheldon. We have been on the
go ever since we arrived from New York."

Finally my mom said something. "Milk and
sugar, uh, Miss, Mrs., Ms. . . . ?"

"Ms. Levine. Bambi Levine. What a positively
handsome fellow you have there, Mrs. Sheldon. We
met outside, didn't we, Todd?"

"Scott," I said.

Finally my mother's tongue started to work.
"Oh, yes, I have two beautiful boys—Scott, and my
baby is Brad."

We turned and looked down at Brad, who had
followed us in. He smiled up at us. But the lady from
the magazine wasn't smiling.

He had taken her bag and turned it upside

down on the floor. My mother stooped to put the things back in the bag, and Ms. Levine patted Brad's head.

Just at that moment, we heard a loud, shattering crash and a scream coming from the living room. Brad was right there with us.

But Malcolm was nowhere to be seen!

8

Star of the Show

Three of us tried to go through the door at once with Brad following.

I saw it first.

It was my mom's powder blue antique vase. Water was dribbling on the edge of the carpet, and the flowers looked like pickup sticks. It wasn't only the cost of the vase, it was the carpet. Everyone got something to wipe up the dirty water. Still, there was a ring on my mom's Persian carpet.

A man with a big belly shuffled up. "I guess it was my fault. Though I don't know what happened. One minute it was on the coffee table, and the next minute . . ."

Ms. Levine took my mother's hand. "Oh, don't worry. We'll pay for the carpet cleaning."

I was beginning to get a headache. I couldn't imagine a whole day of this. Then I saw Malcolm swinging from the chandelier like a trapeze artist. Was that how the vase got knocked over?

Brad saw him, too. He kept looking up and up like he was looking at a skyscraper. Then he started to laugh. It started out as a chuckle. And Malcolm played right into it. The more Brad laughed, the more Malcolm started to show off. He brought his knees up, and then he switched hands.

Brad kept laughing and laughing until he was red in the face and couldn't catch his breath. Everyone was looking at us. My mom didn't know what to do.

One of the crew said, "Happy little kid, isn't he?" Then Brad began to hiccup, and that stopped the laughing.

I slapped him on the back and whispered sharply, "Will you shut up?"

I began to wave Malcolm down, but my mother looked at me as if I was crazy, so I had to stop. Some women brought in the pies. The smell was back in full force. Each pie was decorated differently for the shoot. One had a pitcher of milk on it. Another had a turkey, probably for Thanksgiving. Still another had candles in it, so it could be a peanut butter and jelly birthday pie.

There were tiny pies like cherry tarts. Pies in the shape of stars and hearts, pies with whipped cream and peanuts on top, and slices of pie à la mode. There was another batch with the crust in crisscross strips. Sliced-up pies next to a big pitcher of milk. A half of a pie was peeking out of a lunch bag. Maybe it was the smell; maybe it was all those strangers in my house, but I began to feel dizzy. And seeing all those pies was making me hungry. You'd think that by this point, those pies would make me feel just the opposite.

Ms. Levine said to my mother, "Now, Mrs. Sheldon, if you will just stand over there while we focus our cameras."

"Oh, call me, Jill," my mother said. "This is so exciting. I only wish Jack could be here, but he had to work today."

"Oh, I just loooovve it," Ms. Levine said. "Jack and Jill. How absolutely charming. Our readers will adore this."

Then I heard her say to the man who broke the vase and messed up the carpet, "It will come out of your paycheck, you klutz." I hoped Malcolm didn't have any other funny tricks to keep Brad entertained. That lady didn't sound so nice to me.

"Now, Jill, we want to know how you dreamed up this divine dessert. It's delightfully delectable, divinely delicious, a devastating dash of sweetness."

"Well, I . . . uh, I . . . well, I . . ."

I bumped my mom in the arm and whispered loudly, "Don't you remember how it happened? You kept having nightmares about Blaustein's Blueberry Jelly. You were on this fad crash diet and you were starving to death. They were terrible dreams."

No one said anything.

My mother said quickly, "Yes, so I combined lovely Blaustein's Blueberry Jelly with peanut butter and made the crust and baked a pie. I did it one night."

Ms. Levine clapped her hands and screamed, "Oh, I love it."

Malcolm was swinging so hard, he turned upside down. Brad gasped loudly. Everyone looked at him.

"He's never seen so many pies," my mom explained.

If Malcolm lost his balance, he would fall in or through the coffee table with ten pies on it arranged for photographing. Not that he would make a dent, but he would show up in the photograph if they were shooting. The whole world would see Malcolm in a peanut butter and jelly pie.

This was my mom's big break, and I wanted it to go smoothly. If only I could convince Malcolm to stop trying to entertain Brad. Or better yet, maybe I could just hide Malcolm. I could shove him in the closet and tell him Brad would be okay. Or instead of the closet, I could stuff him under the coffee table. That way, he'd still be a part of things.

And then Brad and I both saw him float down. He settled into the coffee table and ate a slice of pie à la mode with a blackbird on top. He also ate the blackbird. It was made out of licorice.

Brad's eyes were wide. I could tell no one saw the pie disappearing. Especially since the pie didn't look any different sitting in Malcolm's stomach. Then there was his stomach with a neat slice of pie and ice cream and one nice blackbird. The only thing to do was to sit on him until everything about him was invisible.

I stood on the other side of the coffee table and dusted off the legs.

"My, my, isn't that nice," Ms. Levine said, "But, Rod, could you stand with your mother, dear?"

"Scott," I said. If only I could stall. Brad was laughing so hard, he was hitting his fists on the floor.

I moved, and Malcolm was under the coffee table. My best friend, the ghost, was stealing the show.

Ollie, one of the men, took a Polaroid shot of the pies. He waited, pushed the button, and caught the photo when it came out. His face went pale.

"Gosh, there's something wrong with my camera." He played with it for a minute and then unloaded it and put in some new film.

Ms. Levine asked, "Ollie, what seems to be the problem?"

My stomach did double flip-flops. Malcolm waved to me. Brad waved back.

"I have a picture of this old man's face in my camera, and he's smiling."

I heard Ms. Levine whisper about the photographer, "Drinking again. He never got over that last divorce. Wastes a lot of film that way."

Oh no, I thought. Now they would discover Malcolm, and he would be a movie star. Somehow I yanked him out from under the coffee table. Then I tackled him and wrestled him to the floor.

"Scottie?" my mom said.

"I have a lot of energy," I said. "I ate a table-spoon of Blaustein's Blueberry Jelly before breakfast."

"I like this little boy," said a short man sitting in a chair in the back of the room. He was smoking a cigar.

"That's Mr. Blaustein," said Ms. Levine respectfully.

Everyone in the room nodded. Including Mr. Blaustein.

Ms. Levine turned to my mom. "Would you mind if we just did a very short television commercial? It would be shown once or twice. Just for ten seconds."

My mom's mouth dropped open, and she tried to say something, but she just started to stammer.

I'd be the only boy in Jefferson Grammar who had a mom who did television commercials. But then I saw Malcolm standing across the room, smiling. My mom might not be the only person in the TV commercial if I didn't think fast.

Malcolm could show up on television. They'd have a commercial with a ghost in it. True believers and nonbelievers alike would see him. I wondered if the world was ready for this. The commercial would probably sell a lot of blueberry jelly, though.

Someone handed my mom an index card. It was her line for the commercial. I could see she was trying very hard to memorize it, but she was a mess.

"My name is . . . my name is . . ."

Someone helped her along. "Jill Sheldon."

"My name is Jill Sheldon, and I . . . and I . . . and I . . ."

"Maybe the kid should do it," Mr. Blaustein said.

"Take it from the top, Jill," one of the men said.

My mom's face was as pink as her new dress. She just stood there. The cameras were aimed at her like guns. She smiled. Her hands were folded like she was praying.

She didn't say anything. For a long time. It was embarrassing. And frightening. I mean, my mom always had something to say. I looked around the room to see if someone was going to help her. Instead, I spotted trouble. I noticed that one of the cameramen had a strange look on his face. He kept messing around with the focus knob, and then he'd take a step back and look around. I knew what he saw. My mom in her pink dress and this strange old man who looked as though he stepped out of another century.

My mom tried her line again. This time she got it right. Perfect, in fact. I wondered if Malcolm had put the words in her mouth and helped her along. He could do that.

"My name is Jill Sheldon, and I'm the creator of those marvelous Jambutter Pies. You can create one, too. The recipe is on the side of the Blaustein's Blueberry Jelly jar."

"Perfect. That's a take," said the cameraman.

I was glad Malcolm had helped my mom, but now I was going to need some help with Malcolm. He was walking across the floor with a pie balanced on his head.

I zoomed over and held it up so it looked like I was the one who was stealing the show. I don't think anyone saw it gliding in midair.

"Ladies and gentlemen, I have before you a Jambutter Pie. It's an old magic trick of mine."

Brad said loud and clear, "Ghost."

I put my hand over his mouth.

"The kid should do the commercial," Mr. Blaustein said. "He's a natural."

The magazine people were starting to put away their gear. Tears were running down Brad's cheeks, he was laughing so hard. Malcolm had just kept walking through the wall.

I looked around and smiled. Now he was back, riding piggyback on Mr. Blaustein.

It was really funny. It was hard to keep from laughing. My mom just said about Brad, "See, he's in this strange stage. I thought the terrible twos would end, but they didn't. I can't wait until he's four."

Mr. Blaustein came up to me and clapped me on the back. He said, "Son, when you get into high school, come over. You'll find a job at Blaustein's Blueberry Jelly if you want a sweet summer."

With that, Malcolm leaped off Mr. Blaustein's

back and started dancing a celebration jig. Even though I wouldn't be starting work for another four years.

Brad exploded in laughter. He began rolling on the floor, kicking his legs.

"Ghost," he giggled.

"No, no, no," my mom said. "Too much television," she explained to the crowd, who were leaving.

Ms. Levine said, "It's been perfectly charming. I adore your happy little children and your gracious home. Not to mention those divine pies."

Prince II started to rumble.

"Ghost," Brad said softly, and looked up at me. It was too bad Brad kept saying that word all the time. I was kind of glad he couldn't really talk. My parents didn't believe in ghosts. They didn't even believe in horoscopes.

9
Terrible Tracy

I was looking forward to Monday. It seemed as if I'd spent the whole weekend with either my family, a ghost, or some peanut butter and jelly pies. I hadn't seen any of the kids.

The first Panther I saw in the playground was Richie. He was short, and he liked to box. He wanted to become a pro when he grew up. Mostly he would punch the air and box with himself, dancing around.

"Hi, Sharkey," I said. That was his club name.

He looked up at me and kept punching.

"Oh, hi. How ya doin'?"

"Pretty good. What's new?" I replied.

"Nothin' much. We're going to bug the girls after school again. You should come."

"That's funny. No one told me."

"Well, I'm telling you," he said, dancing around.

I had seen the Panthers make the girls cry. I wondered what they would do this time.

Then Blake came up, and he boxed with Richie.

73

Boy, they sure were good. Everyone was watching. I felt someone staring at me. I looked around.

There was good old Howard Fierman. He was looking at me funny. Like I had done something bad to him. I didn't know where to look. I watched the boxing. Then I looked at the ground. But one place not to look was at Howard Fierman's head. Howard had gotten a new haircut. I wondered why his mother punished him that way. It looked like they'd turned a tiny lawn mower loose.

Howard was just different somehow.

Could I help it if I was one of the popular ones?

"Hi, Scottie. What's happening?"

I looked up.

"Oh, hi, Mikey. What's happening?"

I hadn't seen him for a while. I heard he cut school a lot.

"Nothing much."

"Yeah, me too. Nothing much."

"Hey, I heard your mom makes peanut butter and jelly pies," he said. "I heard she's going to be on television."

"Oh, yeah. Well, see, this magazine came to our house and took some pictures, and then they decided to film a commercial, and then . . ."

Kevin came running up. "Come on, we'll be late."

Big Mikey turned to me. "After school. Be here. We're going to let the girls have it. Send them home crying."

Tracy Deevers ran up the steps and stuck out her tongue at me.

The action started at lunch. Blake peeled an orange and started firing the rind at the girls' table. The boys were laughing.

When Rebecca got socked in the nose, she stood up and said, "Stop it. I said just stop it."

She threw half a bologna sandwich across the room. It hit Big Mikey in the shoulder.

He was so cool. He just ate it, and screamed, "Hey, thanks."

Then a teacher walked by, and everyone shut up.

Richie and Blake snickered.

Kevin turned to me. "I heard your mom is going to be this big television star."

"Yeah, she is, but I think she'll still live at home."

We were breaking a record for conversation.

Then I don't know what possessed me. But it was worth a try. After all, they were talking to me. I said very softly, "Listen, do you believe in you-know-whats?"

Kevin stopped eating his apple. "What?"

"You know. You-know-whats. Shh, not so loud."

"I don't know what."

"Ghosts, Kevin. Do you believe in ghosts?" I whispered.

"Why are you asking?" he shouted nervously. "Do you?"

"Of course I don't," I said. "I asked if you did."

"Nah, it's not cool. Panthers have to be cool."

I tried to be cool all afternoon to make up for the fact that I wasn't. My best friends didn't believe in ghosts, but I did. And I knew ghosts were real. They *were* cool. I had one as a roommate.

I tried to be real cool after school when all us Panthers went out together. I was glad to belong. We stood in a semicircle, watching the girls as they came out into the schoolyard. Courtney had on these dark blue high socks that kept slipping down. When she reached to pull them up again, Big Mikey fired the first shot. "Courtney can't keep her clothes on," he yelled.

We all started to laugh. Except the girls, of course.

Boy, that Big Mikey. He sure can think on his feet. I wondered how the girls were going to top that.

"Girls are better than boys any old day. My mom told me," said Babette, yelling until her face was red.

"Babette the Baboon," one of the guys yelled.

Then the boys began our chant, "PANTHERS, PANTHERS, WE'RE THE BEST." We kept it up.

Somehow Tracy Deevers sneaked around behind us, walked over to Richie, reached up, and socked him in the face.

Just like that. No one had even seen her coming. Richie fell flat on the ground. She'd knocked him right out!

Tracy just looked down at him and smiled. Then she walked back to the other girls, leaving us Panthers to stand there with our mouths hanging wide open.

All of the girls cheered, raised their fists, and jumped up and down. Let them laugh, I thought. As soon as someone found out about this, Tracy was going to be in real trouble. Then whose turn would it be to laugh. I couldn't wait.

Big Mikey bent low over Richie, who was lying with his legs out and his arms on the ground. "He's out cold. Someone should get the nurse. Scottie, you go, and hurry up. Maybe he's dead or something."

I ran to get Mrs. MacDonald, the school nurse.

The girls were still cheering. But not for much longer.

Mrs. MacDonald was just about to go home. She came rushing out with me to the playground. I really had to push it to keep up with her. I guess it's because I told her we thought he might be dead. But as soon as we got there, he started to wake up.

"Where am I?" he asked.

"On Mars, stupid," Big Mikey said. He sounded angry.

"Oh, you'll live." Mrs. MacDonald picked up his head. "Well, well, look at that shiner. Got in a fight, did you, Richard?"

I looked at Richie's face. One half of it, over his right eye, looked like a raccoon.

"You'll be okay, sweetie," Mrs. MacDonald said while putting something over the dark part. "How'd it happen?"

Courtney yelled, "Tracy Deevers got mad and punched him."

Mrs. MacDonald laughed. She laughed so hard, she made funny noises in her throat like she was gasping for breath. Finally she stopped.

"Got hit by a girl, did ya?" Then she stood up. "Gotta watch out for those girls."

When she left, Richie fell back on the grass like he was sleeping. The girls started to jump up and down and squeal and clap their hands. Courtney's socks had fallen to her ankles. Tracy Deevers was jumping the highest.

"TRACY, TRACY, SHE'S THE BEST!" They started to cheer. They were joined by some other kids. Howard Fierman stood in the back row.

Big Mikey kicked Richie, and he rolled over on the grass. The crowd parted. The Panthers walked away. But not together. The school bus pulled up, and I ran for it.

Everyone just went home. In the distance I could see some teachers and the principal walking toward Richie. I was wondering what would happen. Tracy deserved to get in some kind of trouble. Maybe she would be expelled. Maybe she'd go to jail.

The girls sat on the bus singing cheers. I was the only member of the Panthers on the school bus. I didn't know where the other guys had gone. I'd taken off too soon, I guess.

When I got home, I ran up the front steps and a second afterward realized that I'd passed a person sitting on them. I turned around.

"Hi! I left after Richie got knocked out and ran home, and then I biked it over here."

Oh, great. It was old yucch-face Howard Fierman.

"Listen, my mom sent me to get a recipe for those pies your mom makes. The ones with peanut butter and jelly. My mom wants to bake some for her bridge club."

"Come inside. I'll get you one. My mom made five hundred copies of it yesterday."

When we got into the kitchen, who should be sitting on the sink dangling his legs, but my friend, the friendly ghost Malcolm. He was sitting in the sink with a bottle of dishwashing soap, taking a bubbly bubble bath with all his clothes on and washing his back with the brush for dishes. Of course, ghosts can't get wet. They can't even get dirty. Maybe it was just fun. Malcolm's friend Napatha liked the water.

"Oh, look," said Howard.

"At what?" I asked.

"There's a ghost in your sink."

"A what in my what?" I said, dropping all five hundred recipes on the floor.

". . . sink," said Brad, dragging his torn blue baby blanket and sucking his thumb.

We all looked at each other.

I shrugged. "Well, it must have come with the house. My dad's in real estate, you know." We began to scramble to pick up all the recipes. "You can see a ghost, Howard?" I thought I'd double-check.

Howard blinked. "I can't see it now."

"Why not?"

"Because it's not there anymore."

I spun around. He was right. There was nothing there. The bottle of detergent was back on the shelf. And Malcolm had vanished.

"Well, maybe I didn't see it. I see a lot of stuff. See, I'm lonely. I probably never saw it. I'd better go home. Now you'll think I'm crazy."

He grabbed the recipe.

". . . Malcolm ghost!" said Brad.

Howard ran out of the house. I knew I should run after him. But that would mean that we might become real friends, and I couldn't do that. Even though he was kind of an okay guy. If only he didn't have that problem with his nose. But if I were friends with him, I couldn't still be a popular Panther.

10

Ghost-to-Ghost

It was sometimes hard to reach Malcolm. He wasn't the kind of friend you could call on the phone, that's for sure. Sometimes Malcolm was around, but he had a hard time materializing. He just couldn't get himself together.

"Malcolm?"

He had just been taking a bubble bath in the sink. Where could he have gone? Howard had seen him. I had to let Malcolm know that.

"Malcolm?"

No answer.

I didn't think he was in the house. Maybe he was outside. I walked to the stable. My dad had finally gotten a horse, a pinto called Eskimo Pie. I liked him, but I was afraid to ride him.

We also had a duck pond. Brad used to think it was a pool. He tried to go swimming in it a couple of times.

I walked down the path back to the house.

"Malcolm?" I yelled. "Malcolm, Malcolm, Mal."

Prince II yipped and ran alongside of me. I patted his sleek fur. He kept looking around trying to find his tail. I figured Malcolm must be close by.

"Malcolm? Wanna play some touch football? We don't have to use your head."

At the word "head," one rolled down the path.

"Hi, Malcolm. I was wondering where you were."

He tumbled out of a big apple tree and put on his head like it was a hat.

"You called?"

"Yeah. I wondered where you were. You were just here taking a bubble bath."

"Oh, I took a little ride to Mars to see some old acquaintances."

"Martian ghosts?" I asked.

"Oh, they're much like our ghosts. There was a purple cat there that reminded me of Napatha in one of her lives."

"Am I up there?"

"You're not a ghost, dear boy. Remember, ghosts can't see people on other planets. Only ghosts."

"Wow!" I said. "It's like a science fiction story. Maybe we could make a movie out of it. We could make a million dollars, I bet."

"No, Scott, my boy. We couldn't do that. You see, the ghosts on other planets are visible until you take a picture of them. You wouldn't see them in a film. It's just the opposite of earthling ghosts."

"Well, no one's going to take your picture down

here unless it's by accident, like at the magazine shoot for my mom's pies. Pies. . . . Incidentally, Malcolm, why did you do all that stuff? You almost got us in trouble." As soon as I said that, I felt angry. And then I felt bad that I felt angry.

"Well, it looked as though brother Bradley was going to have a tantrum if he couldn't be in the picture. The little tyke also had plans for those pies. He was going to turn them upside down one by one very fast. Then where would the picture have been?"

I thought about that.

Then he said, "And incidentally, Scottie, there is someone who can see me. Your good friend Howard Fierman can see me."

"Yeah, Malcolm, I know. But he doesn't know I can see you, and he's *not* my good friend."

Malcolm chuckled, and his head wobbled a little. "I'm not so sure. You have me in common, don't you?"

"Yes, but he has . . ."

"Bad habits?"

"I'll say."

My mom was working in the kitchen and looking out the little window that faced the huge backyard. She yelled, "Scottie, are you okay?"

I had to stop and think about what I was doing. I was walking down the path leading to the house and talking to myself. No one could see Malcolm. In this case I was screaming to myself.

"I'm throwing my voice, Mom. I read this book on how to be a ventriloquist."

Now that the Blaustein's Blueberry Jelly commercial had been filmed, she didn't seem to be on the phone as much.

Malcolm and I ran up the stairs to my attic bedroom. He passed through me and went up ahead of me. When I got to the bedroom, he was sitting in my desk and on it at the same time.

"Why not invite Howard over to play, since we've already met?" he said.

"Hoooowwwwaarrd Fiiieerrman?" I said.

"None other," said Malcolm, smiling, his legs out, his hands over his stomach.

"That's not cool. Then I couldn't be a Panther."

"Then invite one or even all eight of those little animals over."

I was silent. I saw his point. None of them had ever been over except to stand in the backyard. I didn't know where they were now. Playing football? And I thought I was really a Panther toward the end of the party last week.

"Do you want to invite your new friends, Scottie, boy? Or would it be easier to invite good old Howard, who wants to be your friend?"

"I know Howard wants to be my friend. But he's not cool. He picks his nose and eats it!"

"Well, true, that is disgusting," Malcolm said. "But you know, my dear boy, nobody's perfect."

We were silent. This was hard. The Panthers were my friends, but they weren't my friends.

My mom yelled up, "Scottie, are you alright?"

"Yeah, Mom," I said, running to the top of the steps.

Then I ran back.

"I see what you mean about Howard," I said. "But he's just so weird. Too weird. It would be like before I was in the Panthers. I would be friends with Howard Fierman, and I would be invisible."

"I'm invisible," Malcolm said.

I was beginning to get angry. "Yeah, but that's your job. You're a ghost!"

"Sometimes I'm visible. I'm visible to Howard Fierman."

Boy, this was making me mad. "Boy," I said to Malcolm, "this is making me mad. You're my best friend anyway." I thought that would settle it.

I heard a giggle then and watched this little old lady wearing a black dress materialize. She wasn't standing on the floor but somewhere in air.

"Oh, a fight," she said. "I love a good fight."

"Who's that?" I asked.

"Martha, long time no see. How did you get here so fast? Did you try that new-fangled Ghost Express?"

"None other. So this fine young lad must be . . ."

"Scottie," I said. "And you must be . . . Martha."

I now had a thoroughly haunted bedroom.

"I hope you're not here to pick up Malcolm." I said suddenly. If Malcolm left, I wouldn't have any friend I could spend time with and not feel weird. Besides, it was too soon for him to leave. I was just getting used to having him around again. It was great having him to talk to. Really talk to.

"Getting back to your dilemma, Scottie, my boy, do you really think standing in a schoolyard chanting mean things to the girls is that much fun?"

I shrugged. It was, kind of.

"All you do is bully the girls. And this time they won."

"Oh, Tracy Deevers just gave Richie a sock. She'll probably be expelled, and he'll be okay in a few days."

"The girls did that. Oh, good for the girls. What fun!" Martha said, and then giggled. She jiggled all over the way Malcolm did when he laughed.

"Hee, hee. I love it," she said again.

Malcolm laughed. Martha laughed. Then I started laughing because it was just so funny to see them laughing at the same time. Both of their bellies shook like Jell-O.

"Let's get down to brass tacks, kid," Martha said.

Malcolm shrugged and smiled at me. Martha sure was a tough cookie.

"You're still the invisible kid, Scottie."

"Well said, Martha." He winked at her. She winked at him. Then they winked at each other.

"But I'm not the invisible kid. I belong to a club now. Things will get better. They have gotten better!"

But I couldn't think of any recent examples.

"Boys will be boys," Martha said, shaking her finger.

I knew what they were saying. And I knew I should invite Howard Fierman over. He would probably be able to see Martha, too.

Except that I couldn't. I wanted to be popular. I had had a taste of the top, you know. And the guys liked me. I knew they did. It would just take a while, and then I'd be more in the group. I knew I'd be. No matter what, I was still a Panther, wasn't I?

And anyway, I could still be best friends with Malcolm. So what did it matter?

11

Big Scottie

The biggest meeting of the Panthers was held the next day after school. We all climbed the rope steps to the tree-clubhouse and sat down. I stole a look at Richie. His eye was swollen half shut. It looked purplish. He was staring at the floor.

I wondered if he felt like I did. Half there, half not there. The guys weren't talking to him. No one even said hi to him. He seemed more alone than I usually felt. But one or two of the guys said, "Hi, Scottie." I was doing well. The trouble was after they said, "Hi, Scottie," I didn't know what to say.

Patch got up and read the minutes of the last meeting. "Minutes of last meeting," he read. "Scott Sheldon became the new member of the Panthers."

He sat down. I smiled at everyone. No one smiled back at me.

Then Big Mikey said, "Now down to new business. What do we do about the girls?"

Everyone was quiet. I was afraid to say anything.

Big Mikey spoke first. Everyone listened carefully, as usual. They *always* did that when he spoke.

"You know if one of us socked a girl in the face we wouldn't be going to Jefferson Grammar any more."

Everyone nodded.

"But Tracy Deevers knocked out a Panther with her fist, and everyone thinks it's funny."

Everyone agreed.

"So, that's not fair," said Big Mikey.

"Not fair," we all said. I was beginning to get angry. How come no one else at school saw it wasn't fair?

Big Mikey pounded his fist on the table. "Then what are we going to do about it?"

"Yeahhh," we all said.

"Are we going to let the girls get away with murder?"

"Noooo," we all said.

"An eye for an eye," I said suddenly, raising my hand. Everyone looked at me quickly and then looked away. I lowered my hand.

"We have to get even with the girls," Richie said. "We need to teach them a lesson they won't forget."

Everyone nodded and said, "Yeah."

"We could put a mouse in Tracy's lunch bag," Blake said.

"No good," Joey said. "She has three hamsters."

"What about a snake?" Blake said.

"Now, that's good," Kevin said.

We all looked carefully at Big Mikey.

He shook his head no.

I raised my hand again. "Let's take all of Tracy Deevers's clothes when she's in gym and hide them." Immediately I knew it was a dumb thing to say. I never said the right thing with the Panthers.

Big Mikey spoke. He banged his fist on the table.

"Good idea."

"But, Mikey," Richie said, "everyone knows the girls' lockers are off-limits. No boy can get in."

Mikey nodded. "But it's still a good idea."

I felt really good about that. I started to wonder, though, if Big Mikey did that kind of stuff to make me feel better. Or was it to make himself look better? After all, I was his choice to be in the club. If I looked dumb, he looked dumb.

Big Mikey asked if anyone else had any suggestions. Nobody said anything. Then Big Mikey told us what we were going to do, which seemed to be what always happened. "It's not Tracy Deevers we want to hit," he said. "We want to get back at *all* the girls. We want to teach them a lesson. Show them who's boss."

I felt my usual self at the meeting. Uncomfortable. Usually I felt I wasn't good enough to be a Panther. Except this time I felt uncomfortable because I thought what Big Mikey was saying was stupid. We needed a real plan to get back at the girls. But trying to show them who's boss is how we got humiliated in the first place.

Finally, we decided to launch a phone campaign. To call them and call them until they begged us to stop. To play different pranks on them. To make them wish they'd never messed around with the Panthers.

Though I was sure they already felt that way.

Big Mikey got up to leave. And so did everyone else.

I don't know if I got my bright idea then or if it came to me before. But I suddenly thought of a way that I could solve my Howard Fierman problem *and* my problem of not having any real friends within the Panthers.

"Listen, Mikey, can I talk to you for a minute?" I was shaking with fear. "I want to talk to you about something important."

"Yeah, Scottie, that's fine. But I'm kind of busy now."

"Well, when?"

"What about next Friday after school?"

"After school on Friday I go to the dentist."

"Well, what about two weeks from Saturday morning?"

I shook my head. "I might have to baby-sit my brother, Brad."

"Well then . . ."

"Look, Mikey," I said. Again I had the feeling

that some of the ways the Panthers acted were dumb, but I was also scared of him. "Why don't we just talk now? It will only take a minute, I swear."

He looked at me as if he was noticing me for the first time. Usually he looked through me but smiled a lot.

"Listen, I want Howard Fierman in the club. He would make a good Panther."

"Who?"

"You know . . ." My face was turning red.

"Oh, yeah, that's the one who . . . But why would we initiate a guy we make fun of? How would that look?"

"It would look good," I said. "He wants to be a Panther."

Big Mikey began to laugh. I stood there while he laughed. "Everyone wants to be a Panther."

Then he got up to leave.

"There is always the mummy's case," I said. I didn't like what I said, but I felt I had to.

"No one would believe you," Big Mikey said. "I could also kick you out of the Panthers. And then you wouldn't be popular anymore. You wouldn't have the sweatshirt. You wouldn't be one of us."

I thought that I wasn't one of them anyway. I wanted to say, "Okay, then, if you won't have Howard Fierman, I quit." But I didn't. I couldn't say that. I decided to be mean. And think of myself. Because if Howard Fierman was a Panther, I could play with him.

"Mikey, you said no one would believe us. Mr. Macri saw you crying. I could call him up now. He'd back me up. He never liked you."

We stood there looking at each other.

I could tell I'd won him over.

He was quiet. So I *could* prove it. Then he said, "But this Howard, he picks his . . ."

"I know," I said. "Maybe I could tell him not to. He might listen to me."

"But his hair is . . ."

"Maybe he could wear a hat."

"But he's a nerd."

I shut up on that one. I felt pretty nerdy with the Panthers sometimes.

"I can't do it," he said. "He'll ruin the club. Letting you in was bad enough."

That really hurt. *I should just leave now,* I thought. *But that's just what Big Mikey wants me to do.* So instead, I said softly, "They would believe me, Big Mikey, and then where would the Panthers be?"

He was quiet for a few moments, and then he said, "Well, I guess we could make a special exception or something."

"Thanks, Big Mikey. Thanks a lot."

I left him there staring at the floor and climbed down the ladder. I was still afraid of him, even if I did have something over him.

Boy, was Howard going to be happy when he found out he was a Panther. Malcolm would be proud of me. And so would Martha. Maybe now Malcolm, Howard, and I could play.

Big Mikey was Little Mikey that day, and I was Big Scott. Even though what I did to Mikey was a little mean, I'd done something good for someone else. And for me too.

I flew home. I couldn't wait to tell Malcolm. As I was dashing up the steps my mom called. "Scottie, is that you? Come into the kitchen."

I went into the kitchen. She had stopped baking those peanut butter and jelly pies. The smell had disappeared. Now she had a million catalogs spread in front of her.

But I just had to speak to Malcolm or I'd burst.

"Sit down, Scottie. And let's have a little talk. We never talk about anything anymore."

Well, I'd tried.

Uh-oh. The last time she said that, she told me I was going to get a little brother or sister.

"You're still going to have a baby, aren't you, Mom?" I said.

"Oh, yes," she said, and laughed. "But that's months away still. I want to tell you about what I'm going to do now."

My mom put down some warm homemade bread and butter and a glass of milk. But I wasn't hungry. I just wanted to talk to Malcolm.

Just then Brad came into the room. One of his overall straps was falling off his shoulder, and he was wearing only one sock. He looked a little spaced.

"Well, it's so nice to sit with my boys," my mom said.

Then I saw Malcolm materialize. He was standing on his head on the kitchen counter, balancing an apple on his nose. Suddenly Brad giggled. My mom hugged him.

"I wonder what goes on in his little head," she said. "He looked so sad just before."

"Ghost," he said.

I stared at the ceiling.

"Ghost!" Brad shouted.

I tore off a piece of bread and stuffed it in his mouth to shut him up.

"Well, Mom, this has been great, but I'm really busy. I have all this homework to do."

My mom started to cry at that.

"What's wrong, Mom?"

"You're busy, and I'm not."

"But you were busy," I said.

"But it's over. I'm not a star anymore. Maybe there's only one great contest in your life."

"Maybe not, Mom. And you're still a star. Wait until the commercial's on television."

My mom shook her head. "I've been thinking about going back to school, Scottie. I want to expand my horizons. I want to do something more than enter contests."

"Like what?" What could be better than entering contests?

My mom laughed, and finally I got to run upstairs. When I got up to my room, Malcolm was waiting for me, sitting on top of the pinball machine.

"Malcolm, you're not going to believe what happened."

"Try me, my dear boy."

"Big Mikey said he'd let Howard Fierman into the Panthers. I asked him, and he said okay."

"How did you do all that, Scottie? They didn't seem to like Howard the last time we spoke."

"Well, I told Big Mikey he had to take him or I would tell all."

"Would you have, Scottie?"

"Probably not, but it worked."

"Well, I'm not so sure about your method, but your intentions were very good. I'd wager that Howard is a very happy young man right now."

I felt good. I'd made Malcolm happy. Well, sort of. And Howard was probably finding out the good news right now. I tossed the football to Malcolm. "Catch. We won't use your head this time."

If my mom ever saw us playing ball in my room she would have had *my* head. Though if she had seen it, it would have looked like an invisible thing was throwing me the football. To get the ball, I had to hop on my bed, jump down all over my pinball machine, slide on my rug, and tackle my desk. Or so it would look to any outside observers.

I heard Prince II growling from under my bed.

My mom was standing in the doorway. I wondered how much of that she had really seen. She scratched her head. "Scottie, I've been yelling up for a while. You have a phone call."

She disappeared from the doorway just as a football coming from nowhere hit me in the head.

12
The Panther Who Picked His Nose

Running down the stairs, I knew it was one of the guys. I could tell. I didn't get many phone calls. I thought that when I got into the Panthers they would call. But the Panthers were too cool to use the phone. They did things differently. By little notes and stuff.

I picked up the phone, hoping that they were calling to ask me to play football. It was fun playing with Malcolm, but . . .

"Hi, Scott. I don't believe it."

"Oh, hi, Howard," I said with a sigh. I had hoped it would be one of the guys. And then I remembered he *was* one of the guys.

"Listen, Scott," he said, almost whining, "of all the mean, dirty tricks, this has to be the worst joke from you guys."

"Howard, I don't know what you mean."

"Big Mikey called me up."

"Oh, that," I said. I thought something was wrong.

"And he invited me to be a Panther. I have to go through some weird initiation rites. That's a dirty trick if they don't really want me to be a Panther. They just want to have me do all this stuff."

"Howard, I . . ."

"I mean, that's really mean."

"Howard, I . . ."

Boy, Howard sure wasn't used to being treated nice at all. "Howard, it's true. You're about to become a Panther."

Before I said the next thing, I took a deep breath. It was now or never. "But, Howard, I think it's time to stop picking your nose and eating it. I mean, you can make a name for yourself as a Panther, but you have to change your image."

"But I stopped doing that a few days ago, when you told me the last time."

"You didn't, Howard, believe me. You're still doing it. Couldn't you at least cut down and then quit. I mean, now that you're practically a Panther."

"I'm going to be a Panther. Wow! Well, I can't pick my nose and be a Panther. I'll try real hard to remember I'm doing it, and then I'll stop."

"So, when are the initiation rites? Friday? Next week, next month . . . when?" I said.

"I thought you knew. This afternoon, now. Right before dinner." I looked at the clock on the wall. It was only four.

"Oh, yeah," I said, covering. "I just forgot, that's all."

No one had called me. Were they going to leave me out? I never knew with the Panthers. Maybe they just forgot to tell me.

My dad was driving in just as I was running out.

"Hi, Dad," I yelled. "You're home early."

"Hi, Scottie. Going somewhere?"

"Yeah. I have to meet the guys," I shouted.

"What are you going to do?"

"Nothin' much." I was halfway out into the street.

"Okay, then, have a good time. But be home by dinnertime."

The tree-clubhouse wasn't that far away from my house. I ran as fast as I could. When I got there I heard this loud dog barking. I stood and waited for Howard. And then I realized the dog barking was him, and he was standing behind the tree.

"They told me to bark."

"No, later, Howard, that comes later."

We walked toward the garage and the old soda pop machine, covered with dust. Howard got to the lot. Howard barked. Blake came down. He said to me, "Oh, I'm glad you got my message, Scottie."

"What message?"

"There wasn't any time to write secret notes, so I called your house. But your mom said you weren't home."

Wow! They'd actually thought of me. "Lucky I went back in," I said.

"Yeah," Blake said. "You don't want to miss this."

They blindfolded Howard, and he climbed up the rope stepladder to the tree-clubhouse. Someone handed him a sweatshirt, and that was it.

"Welcome to the club, Howard," Big Mikey said. The other seven Panthers sat frowning. Howard reached for his nose, and I pulled his hand down. It must be a nervous habit.

"There's no time for initiation rites, lucky you," Big Mikey said. "We need to discuss the girls. Today. Who's taking minutes?"

We looked around. Todd raised his hand.

"We're going to make them so crazy, they'll lose control," Big Mikey said. Most of the other Panthers said, "Yeah." One or two were silent. Maybe they were mad at Mikey for letting Howard into the Panthers. But what could they say? They couldn't exactly drop out.

"No girl will ever take a sock at a boy again. And that was a lucky punch. Richie was looking the other way. She snuck up. Which is unfair. And it's what girls do. Not boys."

The yeahs were louder this time. Everyone was with Big Mikey. As always.

I stole a look at Howard. He had his sweatshirt on. His eyes were bright and shiny, as if he were in a dream. They had given him his special club name, Booger.

When the meeting was over, Howard and I walked home together because we lived in the same direction. The rest of the guys went in the other direction.

"I can't believe it," Howard said. "Yesterday I was the boy everyone made fun of, and now I get to make fun of everyone else. It sure is great to be a Panther."

I looked at my watch. It was almost time for dinner. I hoped Howard wasn't going to cry or anything because he was so happy. I probably wouldn't get home on time.

I saw a bike heading toward us. As it got closer I saw the long blond curly hair of Tracy Deevers.

"Enemy spotted," I said to Howard.

She stopped her bike, hopped off, and stood there, smiling. She was wearing jeans and her pink satin jacket that said "Pussycats . . . Tracy." She just stood there like she knew she was bad. I waited for the nasty remark. Tracy was good at that.

"Hey, Howard, I heard you're a Panther. What happened, did Scottie get you in?"

That was the zinger. It was a secret club. No one was supposed to know what went on.

Before we had a chance to answer, Tracy smiled at me. She was the first girl to have braces. They kind of glinted off the streetlight, which was starting to shine brighter in the fading sunlight.

Then her voice changed. It got higher. Here it comes.

"That was really nice of you, Scottie. If it's true."

I didn't know if she meant that or was being cool or what.

Howard began to move. His hand reached up, and I smacked it down.

I heard a very quiet, "Thanks, I needed that."

"The only trouble is, Scottie . . ." Her voice got very sweet, not like Tracy at all. It sounded syrupy. I wondered what the catch was. I didn't have to wonder for long. She was ready to tell me.

"The only trouble is I heard that if the girls' clubs and the boys' clubs don't stop fighting, they might not be allowed at all. No Pussycats. No Panthers. But we all know that the boys start all the fights, so it's you who have to stop. And the principal is serious. Think of it. If you don't watch out . . . no more Panthers!"

She smiled and nodded happily.

"Wait a second," I said. "Then there's no more Pussycats?"

She shrugged.

Just then a small wail came from Howard. It stretched into a sound so big I thought it was a siren.

"I wanted to be a Panther. Just my luck. I knew there was a catch. I wanna be a Panther."

We stared at Howard while he had this tantrum. It had been too much for him.

"Howard," I said. "We don't know yet if anything's going to happen to the Panthers."

I hoped nothing would happen to the clubs. There had never been a boys' club like the Panthers in the history of Jefferson Grammar. And there never would again. I wasn't sure there was now. Howard and I were in it.

I got home just in time for dinner, only to find my mom busy again. This time she was getting ready for school. "I decided to audit an adult education course in child psychology," she said. "With you and Brad and the new baby coming along, I may need it. There's a class tonight. If we hurry, I may be able to make it."

I loved it when Mom got really busy, and didn't have time to cook. Then we could have my favorite dinners, like the one we were about to dive into. Hot dogs, hamburgers, cole slaw, potato salad, and for dessert, ice cream sundaes. I hoped she had to go to school every night.

"Hi, son," my dad said. "Did you have fun with your friends?"

I nodded. My mouth was full.

My mom seemed to be studying me. "Scottie, you never bring the boys home to play. Are you ashamed of our house?"

"Hunh?"

"Maybe you want to throw a Halloween party, Scottie? We could fix up the basement with orange and black crepe paper and get some pumpkins."

I shrugged and reached for another hot dog. I didn't know what the Panthers did for Halloween. Maybe they went out trick-or-treating. Probably they had a secret party at someone's house. No girls. If I had a party in the basement my mother would make me invite girls. But Halloween wasn't until October.

Just then my mouth dropped open. Cole slaw slithered off my fork and onto the plate. I watched Brad's hot dog slide right out of his bun and into the mouth of Prince II.

My mom said, "Don't be so surprised. We'd love to have a party for your friends."

Suddenly Brad got up and started jumping up and down, waving his hands wildly.

"Brad loves hot dogs," my mom said. "Should Mommy make you another one? Ketchup or mustard?" She pointed to the two.

"We should encourage him to talk, Jill."

"I'm trying, Jack," she said. "Okay, now tell Mommy what you want, sweetheart."

"Ghost," Brad said pointing to the doorway.

I covered my face with my hand. Here we go again, I thought.

Then I put my fingers in my ears. It was Malcolm and Martha, and they were having a fight. Ghosts can be loud when they're angry.

"What's wrong, Scottie? Do your ears itch? Well, you should wash them more often."

"I do not want to leave yet, Martha!" Malcolm shouted.

Oh, good, tell it like it is, Malcolm. I silently cheered him on.

"You belong on the Other Side. Even now you have trouble keeping yourself together. Your parts won't stay put," Martha insisted.

"Well, they never did. But I need to be with Scottie. He's having a terrible time."

I was, too. Might as well be honest. I had friends and belonged to a secret club, but it was a big secret how friendly these friends were.

"Oh Malcolm, he's just a boy. Boys find friends. It's just a growing stage. Come back in ten years and he won't even be able to see you."

"I have chocolate ice cream with bananas and chopped nuts. Do you want whipped cream, Scottie?"

"I will too!" I shouted to Martha. Of course I would always be able to see Malcolm. He was my best friend, wasn't he?

My mom said, "Well, of course you can have whipped cream. There's no reason to get excited. We've had ice cream sundaes before."

"Ghost," said Brad. He was out of his seat and standing near the doorway, waving his fists. Prince II was alert, his tongue hanging out, panting.

Both of my parents looked at Brad, looked at each other, and then shook their heads.

Then he pointed to the door and giggled.

"Brad just loves chocolate ice cream," my mom said.

But I knew what he was chuckling about. Martha was now about six inches off the ground and still angry at Malcolm. She couldn't seem to keep her feet on the floor.

Prince II sat nearby and just howled.

Suddenly I felt angry. First at Martha for trying to take Malcolm away. And then at Malcolm for having this fight in front of the table.

I could have gotten in trouble. There might have been a slip. As it was, my parents thought there might still be a little something wrong with me and a lot wrong with Brad. Why did the two ghosts have to bring the fight into the kitchen while we were eating? Couldn't they have had it on Mars or someplace?

The worst thing was that when I looked up, they were gone.

"Phoo," said Brad.

"What's wrong, sweetheart?" my mother said. "Don't you want any more ice cream? Let's get down, then, and play." She lifted him from his high chair.

I wondered how the fight ended. Did Malcolm win? I hoped he did because then he could stay and play for a long time. But if he lost and had to go, that would be awful.

Now that I had him back, I didn't want to let him go. I couldn't give up the ghost so soon. Especially since this time, he probably would be gone for a very long time.

13

Giving Up the Ghost . . . Again

The next morning I gave my Panthers sweatshirt the smell test. It would have to be washed. I threw it in the hamper. We weren't even sure there would be a club left.

On the school bus everyone was quiet. Would we lose the Panthers? Would the Pussycats be gone? Would the Triangles in the Fifth Grade have to turn in their T-shirts? Clubs made the school. Everyone who was anyone belonged to a club.

If there were no Panthers, I probably wouldn't even talk to Big Mikey. As it was we didn't say all that much. But I couldn't go back to being the new kid. A no one. Because I wasn't. I was accepted now.

In homeroom we sat in silence as Mrs. Simon read the announcements.

"Boys and girls, let's take our seats. This is from the principal's office. From now on, any boy or girl caught leaving a lunch bag on the table in the cafeteria will have to stay after school.

"There will be an assembly in the auditorium this Friday. Tracy Deevers and Samantha Stone will be flag holders. Girls, please wear white blouses and dark skirts."

I held my breath. What about the clubs? Could we have them or not? I looked around out of the corner of my eye. Big Mikey was biting his nails. Todd was cracking his knuckles, and Blake had turned a paper clip into one thin line.

I wondered what they were worried about. They didn't need a club to be a club. They always hung out together anyway. I needed the club to hang out with them.

Then finally she said it.

"The decision of the principal's office is that girls' and boys' clubs will be allowed at Jefferson Grammar School."

There were loud cheers in the room.

"Unless they interfere with the high standards of the school. There will be no after-school jeering in the schoolyard. No club can fight with, gang up on, or taunt another club. If this is found to be, all clubs will be disbanded, and we all know what disbanded means. There won't be any more clubs. Period."

Every Panther in the room was silent. The Pussycats looked near tears. Half the fun of the clubs was fighting with each other. And when we wore our stuff, we felt more powerful.

At lunch I sat with Howard Fierman, but it was at the Panther table. People were turning to stare.

Someone's mouth dropped open. But I'll say this for Howard. He hadn't picked his nose all morning, and he'd done something to his hair without anyone saying anything about it to him. He looked a lot better.

"Life is so weird," he said.

"Your egg salad is slipping out of your sandwich, Howard, and you have milk on your chin. Not cool."

He nodded and fixed everything. "I mean, yesterday everyone thought I was a nobody, a nothing, and now I'm somebody. I'm a Panther. It means a lot to me."

I nodded. All of that sounded very familiar to me.

But I wished he'd shut up already. What he didn't know and I did was that he was a Panther and he wasn't a Panther. He was in the club, except that the guys considered him one of Big Mikey's good deeds. He'd find out. Meanwhile, I was glad he was happy.

After school I tried to catch up with the guys. There was nothing doing in the schoolyard anymore, and I knew our phone campaign with the girls was cut off. This could get boring. None of the Panthers were too happy. It's like they left the club for us, but took the fun out.

"Hey, Kevin, you want to come over?"

"Can't."

"Hey, Todd, want to play with my pinball machine?"

"Can't."

They all marched across the yard, a sea of gray sweatshirts until Howard Fierman ran across.

"Hey, you guys playing football or what?"

"Can't," they said together. And then they were gone.

On the school bus I sat with Howard. We didn't say anything. I guessed we would see a lot of each other.

It was funny. I got him in the Panthers to make him popular, and now I was going to be stuck with Howard as a full-time friend. Just like before. I hadn't gotten the best of Big Mikey after all. Why did that sort of figure?

"Hi, Mom, I'm home," I said when I got in.

Immediately she looked at my face and said, "You look sad, Skeeter, anything wrong?"

She was back to being my mom again.

"No, it's just that the principal said the only way we could have clubs in school was not to fight with each other."

"Well, that makes sense. Sometimes clubs leave children out, anyway."

She didn't know how right that was.

On the table sat a bowl of bright red popcorn.

"Mom? What's that?"

"Oh, popcorn. I made it with Futz's Food Coloring. Now I have to write a poem about it and take a picture of it and send it all the way to New Mexico. The prize is two weeks in the Grand Canyon."

The Grand Canyon. That was Malcolm's hangout once. They caught him on film, and that's how he ended up in the textbook.

I grabbed a handful of popcorn as I went upstairs. Malcolm. I heard him before I saw him.

His voice was coming from my radio. Mal was an expert at throwing his voice. One time I heard it coming from a banana and another time, from the top of a tree.

"This is Malcolm, the Ghost of Mallory Manor, husband of Martha, twenty-second cousin twice removed of the Ghost of Christmas Past that haunted Scrooge, and the ghost that is HAUNTING YOU!"

I lay back on the bed and flung my arm over my eyes. "You were never related to the Ghost of Christmas Past," I said, "and you know it."

Suddenly he appeared. Or as much of him as could appeared. He was hanging upside down, swinging on the door. I couldn't help laughing.

"Why, Scottie, my boy, you seem a little vexed with me."

He disappeared and materialized again sitting on top of the pinball machine. All of my books in the bookcase showed through him, so he looked like a bookshelf.

"What's wrong?" all the books asked.

I still wouldn't talk.

"Napatha got your tongue?" he said, and laughed and laughed until his belly shook.

"I don't want you to go, Malcolm. Not back to

the Other Side. I want you to stay. You may be the only real friend I'll ever have."

"Oh, yes, I know how you feel," Malcolm said. "But, Scottie, you can be friends with Howard now and still be popular."

I didn't say anything. I was tired of hearing about Howard.

"I think, Scottie, my boy, that there's more. I think you're hiding something. You're lucky. We ghosts can't hide anything from anybody. It shows. Literally. When I get angry I get red. When I feel sick I turn green. Sad, I turn blue. Lost, I'm black, and when I feel happy I turn bright yellow."

"Really? I never saw any of that."

"That's because you're human. And that's why you need human friends. Ghosts come and go, you know."

I looked down. "I'm also mad because you and Martha turned up in the kitchen with my parents sitting right there having dinner. They don't believe in ghosts, but they have two kids who do. And one of them has a very limited vocabulary because of you. Ghost, ghost, ghost. If Brad doesn't learn to talk, he'll never go to school, and then we'll be stuck with him forever. And that peanut butter and jelly commercial. I know you were trying to prevent Brad from getting into a jam, but you got us there yourself."

I felt free. Like I had lost a toothache. Malcolm looked sad, but he didn't seem angry. I went on.

"See, Malcolm, I was afraid to tell you the truth. I thought you'd just leave."

Malcolm nodded, and his head fell off and rolled off the pinball machine.

"But, Scottie, I would have anyway. That's why I'm here. It's time." He put his head back on like a hat. "Scottie, I'm glad you told me. I am truly sorry for any and all trouble my little visit has caused you. You know I never mean you any harm."

"I know, Malcolm. It's just that things sometimes get a little out of hand."

"Darn tootin' it's time," said a voice. We looked up. Martha materialized in the doorway. She was carrying a huge flowered velvet suitcase, holding a lamp with a lavender shade, and wearing a big black straw hat with a pink feather.

"Well, I'd best be off. Found this lamp I left here. There's a Ghost Express coming. I got a round-trip ticket. The last one left two hundred years ago. This one should be here any second. See you later, dear. Shall I wait dinner?"

"No," he said, "This may take a few years. Have a nice trip, dear." He gave her a kiss on the cheek.

"Here I go now!" Martha said and with a *poof!* she was gone. Vanished.

"I guess you want to go now," I said, with a lump in my throat. "It's bad enough being lonely without having to do it all over again."

"Oh, I don't think you're that lonely, Scottie,

my boy. And remember, ghosts continue to haunt. I'll never be far away, even though I'm on the Other Side, wherever that may be."

"Yeah, but I'm losing a friend," I said. "We have fun. And I don't have to pretend to be somebody I'm not."

"Like a Panther."

I looked at the floor.

"Listen, Scottie, you have to say what you mean and mean what you say. So if you have a friend and something's bothering you, you have to be honest. Like you just were with me. Say 'Don't haunt me in the kitchen when we're having dinner.' Or 'Don't lose your head when we're filming a peanut butter and jelly commercial.' You see?"

I nodded. Malcolm nodded, and his head slipped. Then I said, "Like Howard. I told him to keep his hands off his nose."

"Exactly, my boy. Now you're talking."

We were silent. Gosh, I'd hated saying goodbye last time, and I didn't like it any more this time.

"Well, Scott, my boy, I'm off. It may seem like I was here only a short time, but it was about five hundred seventy-five years in Other Side Time."

Suddenly I was frozen with fear. "Malcolm, I don't remember how we actually got you back there last time. Oh, no. You should have hopped the Ghost Express with Martha."

"I can't take Ghost Express. I've been on This Side too long. I can't find it. It's invisible, you know."

"Well, how did we do it the last time?"

"We went out into the backyard, back to the scene of the crime, so to speak." The backyard went for miles. There was almost a forest back there.

Together we marched down the steps. "The backyard," Malcolm said.

"The backyard," I said.

"Malcolm," I said sadly. "I didn't forget. I just wanted you to stay a little longer."

"I may stay a lot longer. The wind is coming from the northeast. That's a very bad sign."

"So it's going to be harder."

He shook his loose head and dropped his left hand. As he searched for it in the multicolored leaves, his head rolled back. He put that back on and laughed. "No, Scottie, it won't be harder. I just said that to spend more time with you."

I wished he could stay until Halloween at least. What's a house with a ghost without a ghost at Halloween?

I bit my lip. Walking together we carefully found the spot where the windmill had stood. It had been built before the house, a hundred years ago.

It was hard to get to the Other Side. You had to imagine it.

"Concentrate, Malcolm. Concentrate."

"I ammmm," I could hear his voice beginning to fade. I paced around some more and scrunched through the fallen leaves. Malcolm paced. I walked through him accidentally and apologized.

Nothing happened.

Malcolm was still on This Side.

And we had reenacted the scene of the crime. He was by the windmill he had fallen from in little pieces so long ago.

A breeze blew through the trees, and I wondered if it would rain later. It might even snow.

I had to concentrate with Malcolm. I tried to picture the Other Side. All I saw was Martha.

I thought and I thought. I shut my eyes tight. I thought how much I wanted to see him home. Even though it wasn't really true.

I opened my eyes, knowing it hadn't worked.

"Malcolm, let's try it a little to the left of that tree," I said.

There was no answer.

"Malcolm?"

Nothing. A bird in a tree cawed.

Well, that was that. He was on his way to the Other Side. That was the end of Malcolm, my best friend, the ghost.

I waved goodbye.

I don't know if it was my imagination or the wind in the trees, but I thought I heard him say, "Goodbye, Scottie."

My mom came out into the yard just then and said, "I was wondering what you were doing out here, Scottie. Why, it's so cold, it feels like snow. I thought I heard you talking to somebody."

"No, Mom. Just singing a song I learned in

school." We walked into the house together. I felt sad and kind of empty inside.

The phone rang when we got in the door.

My mom answered. I was on my way upstairs. "Scottie, phone for you," she said.

"Hi, Howard," I said.

There was a laugh that was almost a cackle on the line, "Hi, Scottie. This is Tracy Deevers."

I only knew one Tracy. No use rubbing it in.

"Listen," she said, "I'm having a Halloween party, and my mother said I had to invite you. Can you come?"

"Gee, I don't know. Halloween is so far away."

"Just say yes or no, Scottie. We have to know how many people can come."

"Yeah," I said. "I'll come to your Halloween party, Tracy."

I saw my mom. She was washing the dishes and smiling.

Next I dialed Howard to see if he could come over and play.

ABOUT THE AUTHOR

JUDI MILLER wrote *Ghost à la Mode* in response to the many letters she's received from kids who loved *Ghost in My Soup* and who wanted to know what happened to Scott, Malcolm, Big Mikey, and all the other characters (real and ghostly) in Chagrin Falls. Judi has also written books for adults and teenagers, including *Figuring Boys Out* and *Boys Talk About Girls, Girls Talk About Boys.* Judi lives in New York City, where she is hard at work on her next book for Bantam Skylark Books, about a vampire . . . named Murray.

Bewitching
new series!

Get ready for teen magic with

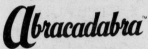

by Eve Becker

ABRACADABRA mixes magic with middle school for an unbeatable new series you'll love! Dawn has always been an ordinary girl. That is, until the summer before eighth grade when Dawn discovers she's inherited magical powers. Only her cousin Jennifer knows the secret—and together the two are going to have their best year yet! Get ready for spells that backfire, mysterious love potions, bewitching fun and more!

☐ 15730-2 THIRTEEN MEANS MAGIC #1 $2.75
☐ 15731-0 THE LOVE POTION #2 $2.75

<u>Prices and availability subject to change without notice.</u>

Bantam Books, Dept. SK38, 414 East Golf Road, Des Plaines, IL 60016

Please send me the books I have checked above. I am enclosing $_____ (please add $2.00 to cover postage and handling). Send check or money order—no cash or C.O.D.s please.

Mr/Ms _____

Address _____

City/State _____ Zip _____

SK38—10/89

Please allow four to six weeks for delivery.